INDELIBLE

Visit us at www.boldstrokesbooks.com

By the Author

Edge of Darkness

Chaps

Split the Aces

Indelible

INDELIBLE

by
Jove Belle

2010

INDELIBLE

ISBN 10: 1-60282-194-1
ISBN 13: 978-1-60282-194-1

THIS TRADE PAPERBACK ORIGINAL IS PUBLISHED BY
BOLD STROKES BOOKS, INC.
P.O. BOX 249
VALLEY FALLS, NY 12185

FIRST EDITION: DECEMBER 2010

CREDITS
EDITOR: SHELLEY THRASHER
PRODUCTION DESIGN: STACIA SEAMAN
COVER DESIGN BY SHERI (GRAPHICARTIST2020@HOTMAIL.COM)

Dedication

For Tara, who takes care of us all every day. I love you.

CHAPTER ONE

Saturday, July 11

Luna arched her back, stretching the muscles and releasing the tension built up over the past forty-five minutes. She inspected her work, taking the image in as a whole. It was good. With the buzz of the tattoo gun in her ear and the ink flowing, melding with the flesh, she never saw the whole picture, just the fluid transfer of color one needle point at a time.

"One more session and we'll be done." Luna disconnected the needle and dropped it into the sharps container.

"I could go longer today." Her client smiled. Luna knew from experience that, for some clients, getting a tattoo was a walk on the wild side and an opportunity to show off to friends.

"It's not a good idea," Luna said. The chair was already booked for another client. "Let's get together in another week, okay?"

She collected her payment, waved good-bye to her client, then dropped her head onto the counter. It hit with a satisfying thunk. Her head hurt, and not just from the blunt-force trauma of cranium meeting table.

"Tell me why I keep taking clients like her?" Luna always felt the sting of artistic sacrifice after a session with Susan. No matter how much ink she added, Susan would never truly understand the beauty of altering the landscape of her body. For her, it would always be a trendy rebellion intended to upset her parents, rather than the affirmation of life that Luna wanted it to be for all her clients.

Her apprentice, Perez, smiled wickedly. "Virgin flesh?"

"We need a bigger space." A larger location would mean more chairs and fewer visits from women like Susan. Her session wouldn't have to be cut short in order to vacate the one and only chair for another client.

"Indeed." Perez placed a fresh cup of black coffee next to Luna. "Drink." She took a sip from her own cup.

"Thanks." Luna closed her eyes and inhaled the aroma—dark, slightly bitter, and so seductive. Perez was a goddess with a coffeemaker.

Luna took a small drink and the ritual relaxed her. "Eventually we'll have to go through all the real-estate listings." She nudged the neglected stack of papers next to the register.

"Yep." Perez took another drink of coffee. She resisted the paperwork involved in relocating Coraggio as much as Luna did. Besides, her client was due in ten minutes, so Luna could forgive her for not diving in.

Like a well-timed distraction, Ruby shuffled across the room above them. About time, too. Luna thought Ruby might sleep all day. Of course, she had good reason, since Luna had kept her up most of the night before. The two of them had an ongoing challenge: who could make the other one scream the most. Luna was determined to win. Besides, Ruby didn't have any other obligations. She was a trust-fund baby, living off the fat bank account that the hard work of previous generations had created. She was a lay-about, though a *hot* lay-about, and Luna could live with that.

Coraggio's current location had one advantage—the living space above the tattoo studio. When Luna first started out, not having to pay rent on an apartment had saved her from going bankrupt. "Ruby's up."

"Ruby's more than up, lover." Looking every bit the femme fatale from a 50s pulp-fiction novel, Ruby appeared at the top of the stairs. She smoothed the fabric of her fuck-me red dress as she descended, one languid step at a time.

Perez scooped up her papers, grumbled under her breath, and escaped to the back room.

"She's still scared of me?" Ruby ran a manicured nail—polish matched to her dress and her name—across Luna's cheek.

"Must be." It was easier to agree than to tell Ruby that Perez didn't like her. Rather, she didn't like Ruby's role in Luna's life. Perez wanted Luna to meet a nice girl, settle down, and raise 2.2 kids. Luna wanted that, too, but she wasn't interested in being celibate until it happened. Wasn't it enough that she no longer considered it a personal obligation to have sex with every lesbian in the greater Portland metro area? Ruby was the perfect solution for Luna—wild as hell in bed, didn't believe in the word *no*, and wasn't looking for long-term commitment. Which worked well since Luna couldn't offer one, at least not with Ruby. All in all, it was a win-win situation.

"You *still* working on this?" Ruby flipped through Luna's real-estate listings. She looked as though something sour had crawled inside her mouth and died there, and her normal honey-smooth voice cracked around the edges. Moving Coraggio seemed frivolous to her. Why fix it if it ain't broken? Ruby obviously did not inherit her family's go-forth-and-conquer attitude when it came to business.

As much as the process for expanding intimidated Luna, a large part of her—the foot-stomping, I-can-do-it part—wanted to prove to Ruby, and herself, that she could make this transition successfully. More than that, though, she needed to remind herself where Ruby fit. She was not her business partner, and Luna did not need to justify her decisions regarding Coraggio to her. Ruby was a fun time in bed, nothing more. Luna wanted to keep it that way.

Luna pulled Ruby in for a hard, brief kiss. As far as distractions went, slipping her tongue between Ruby's teeth usually worked. It not only side-tracked Ruby, but usually left Luna wondering why she was trying to distract Ruby in the first place.

"Coffee?" Luna started toward the back office.

"No, you stay here. I'll get it." Ruby rolled away from Luna, her hips leading and the rest of her body following languorously. "Let's see if I can chase Perez out of another room."

A few moments later Perez scurried in, like a puppy scrambling to avoid Cruella's reach. "Devil woman," she muttered at the beaded curtain, then turned toward Luna. "I don't get it. What do you see in her?"

"You're kidding, right?" Anyone with eyes could see why Luna was attracted to Ruby. Her appeal was all on the surface for everyone to enjoy. She was the perfect stiletto to Luna's combat boot.

"I know she looks good, but what about at the end of the day?"

That question was even more absurd. "At the end of the day she *feels* good." God, did she ever. Ruby could do amazing things with her body, and her buttermilk-smooth skin could almost make Luna forget that she didn't love her. But the moments after climax when reality slammed into focus made Luna want more than Ruby offered. Perez's questions were right on target. Luna wouldn't be satisfied with a surface-level relationship forever, and no matter how hard Ruby made her come, and vice versa, they weren't in love with one another.

"You're hopeless."

Hopeless? Such a final word, which left Luna emotionally tired. She had officially hung up her whoring-around shoes, metaphorically speaking. Still, it was impossible to go from race car to minivan overnight. Transitions like that happened by degrees, right?

"It's not like you're all tied up, Perez. When was the last time you went on more than two dates with the same woman?"

Perez wrinkled her nose and stuck out her tongue. "That's not the point. I'm still young." At twenty-six, she was closer to thirty than twenty, but Perez hadn't grasped that youth was rapidly departing.

Luna remembered the Peter Pan feeling of her mid-twenties. She had held on to it well past her thirtieth birthday.

"And I'm not?"

"You're thirty-three." Perez said the number with a frown. "At a certain point, you really should settle down."

"This conversation is over."

Perez started to speak.

"Ruby is thirty-four. Want me to tell her you think *she's* old?"

The color drained from Perez's face. "No."

They looked through real-estate listings in relative silence while waiting for Perez's appointment to arrive. The sound of Ruby riffling through the morning paper as she drank her coffee filtered in and mixed with the occasional flipping of pages as Luna and Perez sorted, considered, and discarded potential locations.

Frustrated and contemplating leading Ruby back up the stairs for a reminder of why she kept her around, Luna rubbed her hands over her eyes and forced herself to exhale. A tiny bit of tension escaped with the breath and she thought again about taking up meditation, even if it was so damned boring to do.

"You need a nice girl like her." Perez indicated a woman passing on the sidewalk outside.

The woman paused, face to the late-afternoon sun. Her hair fell around her shoulders, light drifting through the blond strands like a movie-perfect halo, and Luna wanted to trace the light dusting of freckles on her cheeks with her fingers. She imagined her shoulder—a crisp white cotton sheet falling around it—sun-kissed and dappled with freckles, each one begging to be kissed.

Before Luna could fall into the fantasy completely, Ruby stepped between her and Perez, steaming mug of coffee clutched in both hands.

"Yummy," she purred. "In a pearls-and-angora kind of way."

Luna mentally growled. Not that she didn't agree with Ruby, but she was not in the mood to share. Naughty thoughts were best savored alone, then acted out with willing partners. She was still in the savoring stage and not yet in the mood to act it out with Ruby.

Another woman who wore tighter clothes and aggressive makeup wrapped her arm around Luna's dream lover's waist and squeezed her middle. They laughed together for a moment, then continued their walk.

The first woman was soft lines and Betty Crocker wholesome. The second looked the type to corrupt even the most innocent of the girl-next-door brigade. Luna wanted to intervene. She wanted to be the one doing the corrupting. Odd that she was jealous of an unknown woman separated from her by a sheet of storefront glass, but not of Ruby's obvious interest. Despite the lack of emotional ties, they had a working commitment. They were casually exclusive.

"I'm heading out." Ruby kissed her on the cheek. "See you later tonight?"

"Mmm-hmm." Luna nodded. Her last appointment was scheduled for nine thirty that night. She was adding gold and blue to a full sleeve she had inked in the previous week. She planned to be done in an hour, an hour fifteen, tops.

Luna watched Ruby walk away, captivated by the generous sway of her hips.

"Focus." Perez smacked her with a rolled-up property listing. "Coraggio won't move itself."

Luna put away her daydreams and picked up the stack of property listings. Only four more inches to sort through. Then the business plan. Then the loan application. She dropped her head to the table again. At this rate, the only thing to progress would be the size of her headache.

Monday, July 13

"It's seriously disturbing to watch you eat that thing." Angie Dressen wrinkled her nose before she carefully licked her nonfat frozen yogurt—the boring, safe cousin to Tori's calorie-laden, sugar-coma-inducing treat.

Tori swept her tongue over the ice cream, collecting as much as possible. She waggled it at Angie before pulling it into her mouth with a loud slurp. "If it's so disturbing, you shouldn't watch."

"But, honey, you know I like to watch." Angie gave her best lascivious grin, complete with jiggling eyebrows. Since this was all the action she was likely to get tonight—or any other night, at the rate she was going—she wanted to make the most of it.

"Baby, I'll let you do more than watch." Tori's voice dropped to an indecently seductive level as she moved closer to Angie.

Tori's blatant sexuality used to shock Angie, even made her drop her frozen yogurt completely the first time she said something so overt. Now it just made her laugh. "Ain't never gonna happen."

Tori shrugged and took another long swipe of vanilla, letting her tongue linger.

"You have plans for this weekend?"

So they'd moved on to polite conversation already? Usually it took a little longer for them to reach this point during their walk. After all, Tori knew the answer to her question. Angie didn't have plans. She never had plans beyond working, hanging out with Oliver, and trying to put a dent in her ever-growing list of chores around the house. "Not so much. You?"

"Could be." Tori peered over the top of her sunglasses at a passing woman wearing ass-hugging shorts and a barely there baby-doll tee. She stopped walking and turned to watch the woman until she disappeared into the next building. "Nice."

Angie agreed. The woman had obvious charms, but what was the point of looking if she couldn't explore further? "You have a date?"

Tori pushed her glasses back into position. "If I get lucky, yes. I'm going to the E Room. You should come."

Tori invited Angie dancing every weekend and Angie always declined. "You know I can't."

Tori took another bite of ice cream. She was down to the cone. "Come on, Angie, by the time you get home, Oli's already in bed. He won't know the difference if you're a couple hours later."

No, she supposed he wouldn't. But she would. Her priority since the day Oliver was born had been to be a good mom, not have a good time. She did date occasionally, but the pickup world that Tori lived in was so far away from Angie's reality, she could barely imagine it. "I can't. It's not a good idea." Angie finished her yogurt and tossed the cup into a street-side trashcan. Tori's ice-creamless cone followed.

"We're almost there." Tori pointed at the business to their left.

"Are you *sure* you want to do this?" Angie paused at the far edge of the building. If they didn't enter Coraggio, then Tori wouldn't be able to do anything stupid. They walked past this building twice a day, but yesterday was the first time Tori had showed any interest in the business itself. Suddenly she was rushing to get a tattoo.

"Yes, for the millionth time, I'm sure." Tori grabbed Angie's arm and dragged her the last few feet. Without releasing her hold, Tori wrenched open the door and urged Angie none-too-gently through the opening. "Come on."

"I just don't get it." Angie looked around the small shop. *Coraggio* was painted in loose flowing script across one wall. Line drawings and pictures of fresh tattoos covered every available surface. "Why would anyone *want* a tattoo?"

"I can think of a couple of reasons." A woman with long, untamed, curly brown hair stood against the customer side of the counter, one hip resting comfortably against the edge. Her legs, lean and encased in supple leather the same color as her hair, were crossed at the ankles.

She smiled, the barest hint of a dimple popping out, and said, "I'm Luna." Her gaze lingered on Angie, a sexy, slow appraisal.

Angie never realized leather pants could look that good outside of the movies. She subtly ran her hand over her mouth. Rather, she hoped she was being subtle, but how covert can one really be when checking for drool? She forced herself to take a steady breath and wondered how many tattoos Luna had. The only visible one was an angel on her right bicep. Rather than the soft, glowing angels Angie remembered from her brief stint at a Catholic grade school, Luna's was in stark relief, bold with hard lines and sharp angles.

A second woman stepped around the counter, wearing just as much leather and more tattoos than Luna. "And I'm Perez."

"I'm Tori." Tori shook Perez's hand, clinging a little too long in typical Tori fashion. She was quick to decide what—or who—she wanted, and just as quick to make it known. Angie envied her that ability. Tori threw an arm around her shoulders and squeezed. "This is Angie." She nudged Angie toward Luna.

"Hi." Angie wasn't sure what to do. What was appropriate tattoo-parlor etiquette? Should she offer to shake hands? Bump knuckles? Grunt? She settled on a shy finger wave and immediately felt like an idiot.

Luna's smile was like the hot sun on cool, fresh-from-the-swimming-pool skin, and Angie was captivated. She wanted to bask in this woman, which shook her. She usually kept her emotions tight to her chest. Extreme, immediate reactions didn't fit into her stable, workaday life.

"I bet you'd look great with a tattoo." Luna gestured toward the drawings on the wall and moved closer to Angie—close enough to touch.

"Uhm" was all Angie managed.

Luna took a hold of Angie's hand, turned it palm up, and traced a circle on the inside of her wrist. "This is a great spot for a small, intimate tattoo. Something special, perhaps?"

Angie shivered. Between Luna's captivating smile and her touch, Angie was trapped. She knew she should step back or respond. Anything. But she was completely vapor-locked. She just wanted to dip her tongue into the dimple on Luna's left cheek. Every well-thought-out argument against tattoos evaporated with the heat of Luna's gaze.

"Or maybe here?" Luna's voice dropped to a lower register. Already whiskey rough, the tone promised all manner of naughty fun. She didn't release Angie's hand as she ran her fingers over the defined edge of Angie's bicep.

Angie's brain misfired, and she barely registered the sound of someone entering from the back room.

Luna released Angie. She took a step back and smiled—a sexy smile that melted a place Angie had all but forgotten about.

"Hello, lover." The woman had brown hair so dark it was almost black, cut in a perfect hard-lined bob. After she stole into the room and wrapped her arm around Luna's waist, she stared at Angie, her eyes flashing with unmistakable jealousy. Angie got the message loud and clear. "You almost ready?"

"I'm not sure." Luna gave the woman a brief, yet excessively intimate kiss. "Give me a few minutes and I'll let you know."

Angie's rush of envy was followed by relief. Luna had a girlfriend. The temptation was off the table.

The woman looked at Tori and Angie, her gaze lingering on Angie. "Well, if it isn't June Cleaver in the flesh," she purred, the words half threat, half invitation.

"June Cleaver?" The assessment torqued Angie. Yes, she looked like every other soccer mom she'd ever met, but she wasn't the one wearing pearls. The woman clinging to Luna had a string of obviously fake ones around her neck. Big and gaudy, they rested between the broad red lapels that framed her neck. Her shirt was open several buttons past decent, and her skirt, with its wide matching belt, swirled around her legs a la sexy pinup girl. She looked like the quintessential 50s housewife on porn.

"Honey, I didn't say it was a *bad* thing." The tone of her voice assured Angie that she thought it was terrible.

"Ruby." Luna placed a restraining hand on Ruby's arm.

Angie swallowed a growl. She didn't know what upset her more, Ruby's—her name was a perfect match for her cultivated harlot look—tone or Luna's physical proximity to Ruby.

"Don't make me wait too long, lover." Ruby dragged a finger over Luna's shoulders, prolonging contact as she eased away, finally disappearing into the back room.

"I apologize about that. Ruby can be a little…overbearing." Luna's smile was sad around the periphery. "Now, about that tattoo?"

Tori checked back in to the conversation. "It's for me." She had been simply staring back and forth between Angie and Ruby, with the occasional glance at Luna. Watching Tori's head move from person to person was making Angie dizzy, and she wasn't even the one switching focus rapidly.

Tori and Luna ironed out the business details, confirming design choice and colors, and Angie listened, unsure if she should intervene. Tattoos—or any other permanent alteration to her body—made no sense. It wasn't like Tori would be able to trade it out for an updated version in a few years.

"Wait." Angie had to make one more plea. She loved Tori too much not to do that.

"Ang, we've been over this." Tori patted her arm. "Just hold my hand and tell me distracting stories."

"But it's just so…*permanent*. Think about when you're sixty. What starts out now as a cute little pink teddy bear will look like a wad of bubble gum stuck to your ankle in thirty years."

Luna arched an eyebrow, folded her arms across her chest, and quirked her lips into the cutest half smile. Her eyes said *I dare you*, but her mouth remained silent. She waited for Tori's response.

"First, I'm not getting a pink anything. Second, I'll deal with sixty when I get there."

"Fine." Angie didn't think it was fine at all.

"Good." Tori took Angie's hand and said to Luna, "Let's do this."

Bob Marley's "I Shot the Sheriff" played softly in the background, and it reminded Angie of every time she'd come home to find her father and his current girlfriend getting stoned at the kitchen table. She'd made the rounds through the house opening windows and doors, trying to air the place out, and learned early on that her homework came out for shit if she did it with a contact high.

Angie looked around for the familiar signs that someone had recently smoked up and thankfully found nothing. The last thing Tori needed was a stoner leaving an indelible fuck-up on her arm.

"I'll watch the front." The way Perez's eyes lingered on Tori said she'd rather watch her instead.

Angie considered offering to trade places. The thought of a needle entering and exiting Tori's skin in rapid-fire procession made Angie feel a little green. She'd much rather hang around out front and warn people away from a similar fate.

Luna led them to a semiprivate area that held a barber chair and a rolling cart filled with supplies. "This seat is for you." As she waited for Tori to sit she said, "You need to lose the shirt if you want a tattoo on your shoulder."

Tori sloughed off her shirt without hesitation. "Now what?"

For the moment, her over-the-top eagerness amused Luna. Time would tell if she deserved the ink Luna was about to give her. It also didn't hurt that she'd brought along some total eye candy for moral support, which was a mystery to Luna. First, Tori obviously didn't need someone to hold her hand through this procedure. She clearly knew what she wanted. And second, her friend was not a fan of body art, a flaw that Luna was willing to forgive providing that Angie continued to look good and stay quiet.

"Sure about this?" Luna selected the black ink and slipped the protective covering from the needle. "We're about to hit the point of no return."

Angie paled, but didn't protest. Luna was impressed.

Tori nodded. "I'm positive."

Luna pushed the button, relaxing with the snick-click as the gun engaged. The low-grade hum as the needle pistoned in and out comforted Luna, the sound so engraved in her routine that the stresses of life receded when she heard it. She let her hand have its way, guiding the needle across Tori's skin with easy, steady progression.

"Angie, sweetie, I need you to let go of my hand." Tori's voice sounded strained, and Luna paused.

"Everything okay?"

"Will be when I get Angie to turn loose."

Angie gripped Tori's hand, her knuckles white with the pressure. She stared at Tori's shoulder with her mouth slightly open. Finally she looked and jerked her hand away from Tori's. "Sorry," she mumbled. "Didn't realize."

Tori shook her hand out. "It's okay. Nothing a little minor surgery can't correct."

Luna resumed her work. "Angie, tell me why you came with Tori today."

"She asked me to." Angie's gaze was again riveted to Tori's shoulder.

"I figured you'd see it's no big deal and get one with me."

Angie shook her head and backed up quickly. "Nuh-uh."

"Stop being such a baby. It doesn't hurt at all." The tremor beneath Luna's fingers belied Tori's casual dismissal of the pain, but other than that, she hid her discomfort well.

"You're not wearing a tank top at my house ever again."

"You've got to be kidding me."

Luna didn't think Angie was kidding at all.

"The last thing I need is Oliver asking for one of those."

The mention of a male who obviously shared Angie's home piqued Luna's interest. Angie gave off distinct dyke vibes, so who was the mystery guy? Maybe she was a bi-curious lesbian-virgin desperate for Luna to turn her out. She'd given up playing tour guide years ago, but the thought was full of sexy possibility.

"He's seen tattoos before, Angie."

"Well, he's not allowed to see yours."

"Who's Oliver?" Luna immediately wanted to take her question back. She was not a part of their conversation and had no right to interject herself into it.

Angie looked away from Tori's shoulder, the constant progression of black ink into tanned skin, and met Luna's gaze for the first time since entering the work area. She regarded Luna for a moment, then said, "My ten-year-old son."

She didn't look away, seeming to wait for *something*, but Luna didn't know what that might be. What could she possibly say? "Oh." Anything would have been better than such an insipid reply.

Angie smiled slightly and sat in the guest chair, no longer watching

Luna work. Luna scrambled mentally for something to correct her blunder, to take away the look of disappointment from Angie's face.

"Ten? How old were you when you had him?" Luna asked.

"Too young," Angie answered. Her voice was flat, but her eyes flared. She obviously didn't like the subject.

"Oh." For the second time in as many minutes, Luna was at a loss. She didn't know what to say and didn't understand why she cared. Yes, Angie was hot, and terribly sweet to stay with her friend in a situation that obviously made her uncomfortable. She was also acting like the worst kind of tourist in Luna's world: narrow-minded, judgmental, and vocal about it. Another white-bread American mom who thought she was above it all.

"At any rate, it's not like he hasn't seen tattoos before," Tori said. "Sandy has at least five."

"That we can see." Angie didn't sound impressed.

"Right, so why the objection?"

Angie sighed. "He looks up to you."

Luna forced herself to continue working, focusing on the emerging pattern before her rather than the off-limits woman with a child at home and full measure of baggage to go with it. Not to mention her vanilla hang-ups about Luna's passion. She acted like getting a tattoo was the first step in a rapid descent to hell and that her son would be able to run out and get a tattoo by himself tomorrow. Luna snorted. *Yeah, right.*

"What do you think, Luna?"

"What?" Luna switched guns, selecting purple next. "Don't drag me into the middle of this."

"There is no middle. Just tell Angie she's acting like she's a ninety-year-old nun and she needs to get over it."

Luna laughed. She'd thought plenty of things about Angie in the past forty-five minutes that would earn an endless amount of Hail Marys and Our Fathers, but none of them included Angie wearing a habit and ninety-year-old skin. She smiled at Angie, putting her dimples to work for her. Women loved that shit. "She's definitely not a nun."

Heat flooded Angie's cheeks and she cursed her damned fair skin. Even with a tan, she never could hide her embarrassment, or her excitement. She needed this field trip to hell to just be over. Why Tori wanted a tattoo was a mystery, more so that she insisted on dragging

Angie along. The only redeeming part of the evening was Luna, even if she did tattoo people for a living. And despite her flirtatious nature, she already had a girlfriend. Angie better remember that.

She focused on the wall behind Luna's head, blocking out the nausea-inducing noise of the tattoo gun. If she didn't look, she could convince herself it wasn't really happening.

"Almost done." Luna's low voice held a soft reverence and Angie glanced over despite her best intentions to resist. The mix of dark ink and blood smeared across Tori's shoulder made her stomach lurch. Luna wiped it away with a gauze square. "What do you think?"

The completed design—a small black-lined triquetra, filled in with purple—was red and puffy, and not nearly as bad as Angie expected.

Luna spun the chair so Tori could see her shoulder in the wall mirror with the aid of a hand-held mirror. "Nice." Tori looked completely pleased, unlike Angie, who still wasn't convinced it was a good thing.

Luna covered the new ink with a bandage, gave Tori directions for care, and escorted them to the front of the store. Tori slipped her shirt into place as she went, moving with careful deference to her sore shoulder.

"Work should be fun until that heals," Angie teased.

"Shit." Tori grimaced. "Totally didn't think about that."

With their transaction completed, Tori zeroed in on Perez, leaving Angie alone with Luna.

"It was nice meeting you." Angie wasn't convinced but saw no reason to be rude.

"I enjoyed it, Angie." Luna grasped her hand with the same intimate familiarity she had displayed earlier, before Ruby arrived. "Maybe we could do it again some time."

Ruby smiled over Luna's shoulder, all predator and sex and not at all friendly. Luna obviously had no idea Ruby was there. Angie shifted, her palm sweaty in Luna's hand, and watched as Ruby slipped out the front door. She didn't know if Luna was hitting on her or trolling for more business. Either way, she *needed* Luna to let go, but she desperately wanted her to continue holding her hand. "Right." She cleared her throat. "Um—"

"Ang, you ready?" Tori stood by the door, jacket in her hand. Angie would bet money that she had Perez's number in her pocket.

"Yes." She tugged on her hand, forcing Luna to release it. Luna resisted, then finally eased her grip. "Bye, then."

Tori grabbed Angie's hand and dragged her out of the shop, similar to how she'd dragged her in. As they exited Coraggio they ran into Ruby, who stood against the wall to the right of the door, exhaling plumes of cigarette smoke out her nose like a dragon.

"You can't have her, you know." Ruby didn't look at Angie as she spoke.

Angie straightened her shoulders and did her best to appear indignant. "She's all yours." She led Tori away from Coraggio—and Luna—and hoped she didn't sound as disappointed as she felt.

CHAPTER TWO

Tuesday, July 14

It felt odd to Angie, sitting at the kitchen table doing homework again just like she did in high school. Except this time around it was all on her laptop, and this fall her son would be sitting next to her while she did it. She'd started her first—in what appeared to be an endless line—college course about a month ago. She hadn't gotten used to the idea of being a student again. Still, unless she wanted to wait tables forever, she had to do something. A business degree seemed a good place to start.

"Taste this." Her dad, Jack, held a wooden spoon to her lips. Angie had to sample what he offered or possibly choke on it. Thankfully, it was usually good. For a while he had decided chocolate should go in literally everything, but he blamed that on a bad case of the munchies. He hadn't done it since, so Angie was willing to forgive.

Marinara, like nothing available in the store, but still lacking *something.* "Basil?"

Jack snapped his fingers, set the spoon on the counter, and wiped his hands on his apron. "I'll be right back." He rushed out to the back deck, his skirt swishing around his calves, and returned with a single basil leaf from his planter garden.

Oliver licked his lips. "Can I taste it?" At ten he was growing like crazy and always hungry.

Angie held out a hand to block Jack from handing the spoon to Oliver. "What's in it?"

Not that a small taste would likely hurt Oliver, but she'd rather not expose him to the wonders of cooking with marijuana quite this young. And with her father, you could never tell. Was he making the sauce for their dinner or to take to a potluck? Old hippies were big on social gatherings.

"Nothing to worry about."

Angie pulled back her hand, Oliver tasted the sauce, and Jack waited. He took great pride in his cooking and his grandson. The boy's opinion mattered. If Angie hadn't insisted Oliver do some reading from his summer book list, he'd be at the stove cooking with Jack.

"Mom's right. Basil."

Jack nodded and chopped the herb. He stirred it in and returned the lid to the pot. "I have a date tonight, but I'll be home for dinner."

"I won't." Oliver threw the statement out casually and Angie resisted a laugh. That was the hardest part about being a parent—holding back laughter when her son said something absurd.

She put on her carefully practiced "mom" face—stern, loving, but no pushover. "And where do you *think* you're going?"

"Rich and I plan to hit the mall."

"You do, huh?" She arched a brow and waited for the theatrics to begin.

Oliver closed his book. "Mom, don't act like it's a big deal. His brother said he'd drive us."

Rich's older brother was a rolling disaster. Someone would get seriously hurt around him soon, or he'd end up in jail, or both. Angie no longer found the situation amusing. "No way."

"Mom," Oliver whined and Angie cringed. She'd take surly and argumentative over whiny any day.

"Don't 'mom' me. I just canceled your plans."

Oliver shoved his chair away from the table with much greater force than necessary. "Fine!" He stormed out of the room, and his bedroom door slammed a moment later.

Angie shook her head. "He makes me tired."

Jack stirred the marinara and shrugged. "He's ten."

"I didn't act like that." Angie remembered being ten. Her father was barely present at that age and wouldn't have noticed a loud door.

"No, honey, you didn't."

Angie wondered if he really remembered. He'd spent the majority of that year half-baked at the beach with a woman named Monica, who painted icons on the sand just so she could watch them wash away with the tide. She claimed to be very existential. Angie thought she was flaky.

"You should probably change for your date." The sauce was simmering and it wasn't time to cook the pasta.

Jack looked at his clothes—the long dress ended just below his knees. Even though she should be used to the visual combination of feminine skirt and hairy legs, she still found it disconcerting.

"Oh, yeah. I forgot." He hung his apron on a hook in the pantry and began to pull his housedress over his head.

"Jesus, Dad, in your room. I don't want to see that."

"How did I raise such a prude?"

His question was legitimate. He was a dress-wearing hippie, a free spirit who let the moment determine his actions. The thought of floating through life like a damn leaf made Angie shudder. She wanted control. She made plans, worked hard, and adjusted. She refused to just let life happen.

"Just lucky, I guess."

Learning that her family was different was a lesson that came in degrees for Angie. Her first day of kindergarten, she came home and asked where her mom was. Jack's answer—"Honey, she loves you and will be back soon"—lost its power when year after year the woman never reappeared. She was long dead, for all Angie knew. Her first soccer game—second grade, Running Hornets—all the other fathers showed up wearing jeans and T-shirts. Her dad wore a lovely skirt and work boots. A friend had dared him and he—in a giggling fit—couldn't resist a good prank. He'd liked it so much it became a habit.

Moments like that curved her view of life. She worked extra hard to be normal, to make up for her father's eccentricities. When she was seventeen, it had been difficult. At twenty-seven, some of the bitter aftertaste was wearing off. She found him amusing.

Angie closed her computer, homework on hold for a case of parenting, and called, "Oliver, come help me make the pasta."

The volume of his stereo increased. She didn't know the song and felt older than usual. Oliver didn't reply.

Angie filled a large pot with water, added kosher salt and olive oil, and set it to boil. Before getting the pasta from the cupboard, she opened the breaker panel located inside the small pantry. She flipped the breaker for Oliver's room and waited.

The music died and Oliver hollered, "Ah, Mom!"

"You can sit in your room in the dark with no music. Or you can come help me fix dinner. Your choice." Angie couldn't wait for Oliver to hit his teens. She'd been told thirteen was the worst, but couldn't imagine him acting out more than he did now.

Oliver appeared in the kitchen doorway, head down and shoulders slumped. He sulked like a champ.

Angie handed him the box of noodles. "What's so important about the mall?" Half of her wanted to just leave the topic alone. Everything was hypercritical to Oliver lately. No doubt he had attached a life-and-death meaning to a trip to the food court. Still, she wanted him to learn to approach conversations rationally, to be able to navigate difficult topics with grace.

Oliver shrugged and poured the pasta in the rolling water.

"Oliver? A shrug is not an actual form of communication."

"There's this girl…" Oliver poked at the pasta with a fork.

It was always about a girl. The same had been true when Angie had sneaked out to meet someone. Except she didn't sneak because her dad didn't keep track. He wasn't home to do that.

"I see."

"So you'll let me go?" Oliver met her gaze, a hopeful, yet cautious smile on his face.

She hated to disappoint. "No."

He gave up poking the noodles and sat at the table. "It's not fair."

Angie wanted to point out that he wasn't old enough to self-supervise at the mall. That, however, would only escalate to an argument about his maturity. Her head still hurt from the last time he tried to convince her that he was practically an adult.

"Son, make a date with her for a different day when I can take you."

Oliver rolled his eyes and snorted. "Yeah, right."

"You're not going with Richie's brother. So it's me or not at all."

"Fine. Whatever."

When he pouted like that, Angie wanted to ruffle his hair. She resisted.

Jack reappeared wearing jeans and a black leather vest. No shirt. He tousled Oliver's hair—Angie was jealous that Oliver let him do it—and said, "Help me set the table, squirt."

As they placed the dishes and silverware, a sweet smile, the one that reminded Angie of her little boy, gradually replaced Oliver's frown. "Grandpa, maybe you could take me to the mall this weekend?"

Jack laughed. "It's possible."

Angie was unsure how her retirement-age father rated as cooler than she did. Unsure, but not surprised.

They ate comfortably together, Oliver's resolve to be unpleasant fading under his grandfather's good cheer. As they finished, the loud rumble of a motorcycle engine rolled into the driveway.

"Sounds like my date is here." Jack was up and out the door, leaving the cleanup to Angie and Oliver.

Angie watched her dad ride away, clutching the middle of a bleached-blond bombshell as she wound her Harley's engine up higher than it needed to go in the short distance from Angie's drive to the traffic-controlled intersection. Sandy took up more space than necessary, both visually and audibly.

"You can finish your homework in your room, if you want." Angie flipped Oliver's breaker back on. "I'll take care of the dishes."

Oliver escaped while Angie was in the mood to let him, leaving her alone.

First, dishes, then homework, and she absolutely would not fantasize about Luna's hands, her laugh, or her long, long legs that started at the floor and went all the way up to her perfect, squeezable ass.

Friday, July 17

Every table in The Cadillac was full, and Angie barely had room to walk from the kitchen to the table of ten rowdy college boys clomping their forks against the table. She reminded herself to smile as she set a plate in front of the ringleader.

"Keep your shorts on, boss. You always in this big a rush?" She channeled the spirit of the stereotypical dive truck-stop waitress. The Cadillac wasn't a dive, but with its trendy use of neon and black light, Angie imagined that was only a few years away.

"Feisty. I like that." The young man reached out to slap Angie's ass. She dodged and continued to place plates on the long table.

"Careful, son, you put your hand where it doesn't belong, it may come back altered." Thankfully, being playfully snarky was part of the package her manager embraced. She could say almost anything—and had—as long as she kept smiling. So far, however, she hadn't tried to break off roaming fingers. She doubted she could get away with *that*, no matter how big her smile.

Angie finished serving the table, then grabbed a large piece of white butcher paper from behind the counter. She folded it into an impromptu chef's hat and wrote *I shave my balls* on it with a thick black marker.

Then she dropped it on the loud college boy's head, kissed him on the cheek, and flipped off the camera his buddy produced. She walked away as the light from the flash dissipated. The table erupted in hoots. "I think she likes you." "I knew you shaved, man."

Angie escaped into the kitchen and her smile dropped.

"You sure it's a good idea to wind them up like that?" Tori asked as she brushed by, balancing too many plates.

"Tip." Angie shrugged. She scooped half of Tori's load out of her hands and followed her back into the mêlée, where she served Tori's table, then made a much-needed dash to the ladies' room.

With her bladder no longer stretched beyond capacity, Angie exited the restroom and ran smack dab into Luna.

"Whoa." Luna placed a steadying hand on Angie's elbow. "Careful there."

"Luna." Angie should have apologized for almost knocking a customer flat. As it was, she barely managed the half-whispered acknowledgment of who stood before her.

Luna's face softened with recognition. "Angie." She didn't release her hold.

They stared at each other for several moments. When Angie

snapped out of Luna's hypnotic hold on her, their faces were several inches closer. She stepped away from Luna. "How can I help you?"

Luna's hand fell to her side and she hesitated. "Perez sent me to pick up dinner."

"Perez?" Angie remembered Perez showing up a few nights ago in search of Tori. The two had been disgustingly flirty. Regardless, she needed to come up with more than a one-syllable answer. She took a breath and collected her thoughts. "I'll get your food." She ducked around Luna.

"Wait." Luna grabbed her arm a second time and the thrill shot through Angie. She couldn't remember what she was supposed to be doing.

Angie stepped backward and Luna advanced, her steady approach counterpoint to Angie's faltering retreat. They continued like that, Luna stalking and Angie shrinking but wanting more, until Angie's back hit the wall. With nowhere else to go, she squared her shoulders and held Luna's half-lidded gaze.

"Angie…" Luna cleared her throat, but her voice remained hoarse and low. "What are you doing Saturday?"

The question caught Angie off guard. Her thoughts were focused on the nearness of Luna's body, the whiskey-rough color of her voice, the ever-increasing field of bumps rising on her skin in the wake of Luna's hungry gaze.

"Saturday?" Angie fought to clear her head. "Why?"

"I thought we could, uh, you know." Luna's stuttered response made her even sexier. "Date. A date. With me on Saturday." She smiled confidently.

Angie closed her eyes and focused on breathing. Luna's scent overwhelmed her—leather and sage. She never realized how sexy the two were and swayed closer to Luna.

"A date? With you?" Angie was a breath away from saying yes when she remembered her obligations. She shook her head slowly. "No, I work."

Luna's smile faltered, then came back full force. "That's okay. We can get together before that." She said it like it was the perfect solution and of course Angie would agree.

"No, my son has a ball game at Custer Park tomorrow afternoon." No matter how much she wanted to spend more time with Luna, Saturday night or otherwise, Oliver came first.

"Son?" Luna's expression went from confident and seductive to baffled in a flash. "I forgot."

And that was the moment Angie knew would come, but wasn't quite prepared for mentally. Being a mom moved her from date material to wife material. For some that was a major turn-on that triggered a need to load up the proverbial U-Haul and move in. For others, it meant it was time to move on. They didn't want to get involved with a single mom. Knowing that Luna fell into the latter category didn't cool the heat between them. It just made it impossible to act on.

"Oh." Despite the disappointment in Luna's voice, she inclined her head closer to Angie's.

Luna's breath tickled Angie's skin, and she held herself perfectly still. God, she wanted Luna to close the gap between them.

Before they could go any further, Tori's voice interrupted. "Angie? Table twelve needs their check and sixteen wants to order dessert."

Life slammed back into focus. She was at work, not on a date. She placed both hands on Luna's chest—God, it was a great chest—and pushed her away. "Stop." She took a deep breath. "Just stop."

Luna stepped back, her face clouded with desire and confusion. Before she could speak, Angie ran past her and into the kitchen. Tori followed closely.

"What the hell was that?" Tori's smile was enormous.

"Nothing." And it really was nothing. Luna wouldn't pursue the situation, whatever it was, after the reminder about Oliver.

"That's one hell of a nothing."

Angie didn't answer as she printed out the check for the boisterous young men at table twelve.

Later, with the check paid, tip on the table, and all his friends outside waiting, the fork-clomping leader approached Angie, the white paper hat folded and tucked under his arm. It amazed her how many people took those damned things home, like a treasure or something.

"Hi." He chewed his lip.

Angie nodded. "Hi."

"Um, listen, I'm sorry about earlier." His smile was slick with practiced frat-boy charm. Angie was certain this act got him a lot of action. "I was out of line."

"Yes." She couldn't stand where this production was headed. How much had he bet his buddies? Was she supposed to follow him to the bathroom and drop to her knees, or meet him after work and take him home? Luna's scent clung to her and the memory of their near kiss was driving Angie crazy.

"Can I make it up to you?" The playful, puppy-dog look was charming, she had to admit. God forbid Oliver ever got this good at picking up women.

"No."

It took a moment for her answer to register. His smile fell. "No?" Clearly he was not used to being rejected.

"See her?" Angie pointed at Tori. "She's the only one who gets to make things up to me." It was a convenient lie that they used frequently. It kept them safe without completely alienating the customer. Their boss liked it. As he pointed out on many occasions, lesbians were sexy.

Tori glided over to Angie.

The boy looked between Angie and Tori. "I don't get it." He was denser than most.

Not bothering with further comment, Angie kissed Tori. Not a quick, could-be-friends kiss. Oh, no. She went full in, tongue and all. Everything she'd wanted to do with Luna earlier came pouring out. Her point had to be crystal clear. She was not in the mood for this boy.

Tori had great technique and Angie wished, not for the first time, for even the tiniest spark. Nothing. She was tonsil deep and didn't feel even a fraction of the energy she shared with Luna in just a glancing touch.

When she finally pulled away, the boy was gone, but several other diners were cheering and clapping. She felt empty and her head was starting to ache.

"Okay, floor show's over."

It was another busy Friday night, which made Angie's feet hurt and taxed her ability to be even fake-cheerful. Thank God, nights like that always passed quickly.

Angie punched out and dove into her purse. Surely she had some ibuprofen in there somewhere. Mint? No. Hairspray? No. Safety pin?

Ouch. No. Angie closed it and put it back. "Aha." She pulled out the small bottle and smiled her first real smile of the night. It wasn't a face-altering, light-up-the-room kind of smile, but it was genuine. She tapped out four of the little tablets. Eight hundred milligrams ought to slay the pounding in her temples.

"Headache?"

Angie swallowed the pills without water and held out the bottle. "Mmm-hmm. You need?"

"No, I'm good." Tori tugged on her sweater and threw her arm around Angie's shoulders. "Poor thing, let's get you home."

They walked together, no small talk, just the comforting presence of her best friend to help with the persistent throb behind Angie's eyes. Angie paused when they reached Coraggio and looked through the window. She wished for an excuse to go in and say hi, but knew she wouldn't take advantage of it even if she had one.

Luna was working on a client, head bent to her work. Her hair formed a protective barrier, preventing Angie from seeing the design or catching Luna's attention. She watched for several moments, captivated by Luna's intense focus. Not that she could see Luna's eyes. They were hiding behind the cascading wall of rich brown hair. It was the way she held her body—controlled, each movement flowing, precise, and tight. No gesture wasted.

Angie's headache didn't disappear, despite the perfect freeze-frame moment. But standing in the soft light that filtered through the storefront window, she realized that though the ache was still there, it just didn't register. In the battle for her attention, Luna defeated the pain.

Luna turned her head slightly, and Angie met her eyes for the first time. Luna straightened, right hand on her client's shoulder, tattoo gun in the left, and held Angie's stare. Her mouth curved in a gentle, unassuming smile, so different from their previous meeting.

She's left-handed. It wasn't an important detail, but Angie added it to the small catalogue of information she had already stored away about Luna.

Angie raised her hand in a small wave and Luna returned the gesture. They stared at one another so long, the moment stretched thin and she finally snapped back to reality. After lowering her hand she rushed to catch up with Tori, who was half a block ahead.

Luna was a fantasy. One that she needed to get over quick. Women like Luna never stayed for breakfast. Angie, on the other hand, was a breakfast, lunch, and dinner-for-the-rest-of-our-lives kind of girl.

The throb in her temple increased with every step.

CHAPTER THREE

Saturday, July 18

The sun was shining, and by the bottom of the seventh inning, Luna had gotten three hits. Granted, one was a foul, but the other two were solid. The first had been a low-sailing fly ball that landed between the players in left field. The second, a line drive, knocked the pitcher flat and pissed off the other team. She felt bad about that, but not bad enough to forfeit her base. She suffered through their jeers at first base.

Three more hitters and it would be her turn at bat again. She didn't expect that to happen this inning. The pitcher was all kinds of fired up after being embarrassed earlier. She hadn't given up a hit since Luna caught her off guard.

Perez sat next to her on the bench, Gatorade in one hand, unopened pack of Marlboros in the other. She nudged Luna with her shoulder and dropped the cigarettes into her gym bag. "You never did say why you came today."

It was a legitimate, if obtuse, question. Luna hadn't made it to a game in weeks.

"Quite the coincidence that Angie's here, too." Perez gestured to the bleachers behind theirs.

Coincidence, my ass. Luna had checked her softball schedule the second she arrived home with dinner the other night. When Angie mentioned Custer Park, Luna knew that the games would be held in the same place. Luck was on her side because they were also at the same time. No way would she miss it when fate packaged it so nicely for her. She didn't understand how Oliver had a game when Little League season had ended a couple of months prior. Regardless, he was playing and, more important, Angie was there watching.

"Is she?" Luna took an exaggerated look at the bleachers. She zeroed in on Angie far too soon to feign ignorance, but she did so anyway. "I hadn't noticed."

"And here comes your girlfriend." Perez pointed at Ruby marching along unaware that three-inch heels and gravel lots do not go together. Her eyes drilled in on Luna, then darted once to Angie, then back to Luna and held. She'd dyed her hair a deep mahogany since the last time Luna saw her and the copper highlights flamed red in the sun, making her look like a righteously scorned woman. "And she looks pissed," Perez said.

What the hell was she doing there? This development would drastically affect her plan to talk to Angie after the game.

"She's not my girlfriend." Luna knew Perez was baiting her, but she couldn't hold back the snapped reply.

"Really? Then what is she?" For some reason, unknown to Luna, it was important to Perez that she define her relationship with Ruby.

"Convenient." Luna lifted the Gatorade from Perez's grip and took a long drink. If her mouth was otherwise occupied, Perez wouldn't expect her to hold a conversation.

"Then why not go over there and say hello to Angie?" Perez inclined her head toward the adjacent field. Angie, along with an older man, was watching a Little League game.

Why not indeed? God knew Luna wanted to. She wanted to ask if Angie felt the same fluttering in her stomach, the same shortness of breath, like her presence eclipsed the whole world. But she couldn't do that. Christ, she'd just described the symptoms of an asthma attack. What would she say? "Hi, just wondering if you develop a chronic lung disease when I'm around. I do, when I'm around you, that is." No, that wouldn't work. Luna was reduced to a babbling idiot in a fictional conversation with Angie. Imagine if she tried to talk to her.

"It would be rude."

"Rude to say hello? I'm confused. Since when are good manners actually bad?" Perez retrieved her drink.

"Not rude to Angie. I'm talking about Ruby." Luna smiled at her non-girlfriend who was almost at their ball field. "Now shut up. I don't want you to upset her."

"You don't want *me* to upset her?" Perez asked. "Look at her. She's not in a sunshiny kind of mood now. What the hell is she even doing here? First you show up, then her. You two are fucking up my game-day routine." Perez, like most ball players, was highly superstitious. Luna thought it was all crap.

"I'll handle Ruby, you worry about your routine." Luna stood. She needed to intercept Ruby sooner rather than later. The longer she was left to stew, the worse her tantrum would be. Ruby redefined high-maintenance. "And for the love of Christ, do *not* say anything about Angie to Ruby."

After the last time Perez mentioned Angie in front of Ruby, it had taken Luna twenty minutes to talk Ruby out of her clothes. That was twenty minutes too long for a relationship based exclusively on sex. Ruby was hot as all fuck, but damn, she could act like a girl sometimes.

Luna left Perez on the bench and jogged over to Ruby at the edge of the field. "What a nice surprise." She kissed Ruby on the cheek. On the rare occasion that Ruby attended a ball game, she always showed up at the very end. She liked Luna all sweaty and pumped up with victory, but didn't want to watch the actual game.

"Weren't expecting me, were you?" Ruby pulled Luna in for a much more thorough kiss. Before their lips met, Ruby looked over Luna's shoulder. Angie's set of bleachers was in her direct line of sight.

The kiss felt more like an assault to Luna, like a small child snatching back her toy without thought or affection for it, simply a desire not to share. When Ruby finally released her, Luna sucked in a breath and tried to smile. Her confusion made it difficult.

"It's still nice to see you." Luna tucked Ruby's hand into the crook of her arm and led her to the bleachers. Ruby liked being escorted like that. It was the perfect accessory to her carefully constructed image. "You can watch the rest of the game, then I'll take you home."

"How much is left?" Ruby pulled Luna onto the seat next to her and gestured toward the field, where the teams were switching sides.

Her anger was dissipating, but Luna was sure it would take very little to get her fired up again. She hoped her steady show of attention—though lacking devotion—would be enough to stave off another burst of steam.

Luna's turn in center field was over, so she could sit with the spectators for a bit. Besides, Ruby was toying with the frayed edge of her T-shirt—she'd ripped the sleeves off her team jersey at the beginning of the season. Her fingers grazed the overheated skin on her shoulder just enough to get Luna's attention. She was ready to call it a game and take Ruby home. Ruby was safe. Luna knew exactly what Ruby wanted and how to give it to her. Angie was a minefield of uncertainty. Luna's attraction to her made no sense.

"It's top of the eighth."

"Lover, as sexy as all that sports talk is, you know I don't know what that means." Ruby was relaxed. The use of the term *lover* indicated that she'd forgiven Luna for any perceived wrongdoings.

Three full seasons of Luna's softball games and Ruby still didn't understand simple terminology. Granted, she never watched the game, but Luna was surprised that not even the basics had seeped into Ruby's brain.

"Two more innings to go."

"And how long will that take?" Ruby inched closer, her breath hot against Luna's ear. "I'm hungry."

Luna could easily lose herself in Ruby's presence, the brush of her breasts against Luna's arm, the promise of fun and debauchery in her voice. Ruby was a master at seduction. Luna forced herself to respond. "Depends. Could be ten minutes. Could be an hour."

"No way am I waiting an hour for what I want to do to you." Ruby moved her hand dangerously high up Luna's thigh.

"Luna, stop dicking around and get over here." The coach's voice interrupted Luna's impending explosion.

She gave Ruby a quick kiss. "I'll be back. Will you wait?"

Ruby poked out her lip in a pout, but nodded.

As Luna trotted to the players' bench, she glanced over to the other field. Angie was staring at her. Hard.

❖

"You see someone you know?"

Angie cursed under her breath and turned back toward Oliver's game. It was bad enough that Luna's presence distracted her so much; she didn't need her father to know about it. In his mind, she was still in high school, and he found an enormous amount of pleasure in teasing her about a perceived crush. She'd smiled a little too big at the UPS delivery driver once and her father didn't let her forget about it for three months.

"No," she replied without looking at Jack. He had an uncanny knack for knowing when she was stretching the truth and no compunction about calling her on it.

"Really? Because you were burning holes through that woman over there." True to form, Jack called bullshit on her white lie. Sometimes Angie wished he would just leave well enough alone.

"I met her, but I don't *know* her." Angie hoped that would satisfy him.

"So, she's someone you'd like to know?"

"Yes." Angie realized a moment too late what she'd said. "I mean no. No." She tried for confident, but the statement still came out sounding a lot like a question.

"Okay." Jack seemed nonplussed. "You realize you aren't making sense?"

"Yes, can we drop it now?" Angie stared resolutely at the ball field. Oliver was covering first base and the runner there was stretching his lead from the plate so far it was obvious he was trying to steal second. She pointed to Oliver. "Watch your grandson."

When Jack returned his focus to Oliver's game, Angie risked another glance at Luna. Her girlfriend was sitting in the bleachers staring at her fingernails. Odd that she even showed up if she found the game so boring. Luna was next at bat and Angie suppressed the urge to cheer. Not that Luna needed encouragement for her batting, but anyone who looked that good wearing a torn jersey and a whole lot of sweat deserved some vocal encouragement.

Angie felt almost guilty about her inappropriate thoughts about Luna, but had decided to let it be what it was: an enjoyable fantasy. Yes, she was objectifying the woman. The feminist in her protested, but the lesbian who needed to get laid could live with it.

Hoots and hollering around her brought her back to the game she had come to watch. A batter from the other team scored a hit, but the outfielder scooped it up and threw it to Oliver.

Angie held her breath as the ball arced through the air. Even though he'd been playing ball since he was five—when he joined his first T-ball team—she still crossed her fingers and prayed every time the ball approached him. He didn't miss very often, but when he did, it was spectacular. The guilt he felt afterward was enormous, and it took days for Angie and Jack to pull him out of it.

Oliver caught the ball with a practiced tip of his glove, then tagged out the runner with a serious smile. That expression always cracked Angie up. She didn't know how he managed to look so happy yet so earnest at the same time.

Half of the spectators erupted into cheers. The other half groaned. That was the final play of the eighth inning and Oliver's team was ahead by two runs. Not a large enough lead to get cocky, but comfortable enough for the other team to feel the early pangs of defeat.

Angie glanced back at Luna's game. Luna had just stepped up to the plate and was mid-swing. The bat connected with a mighty crack and the ball sailed deep into left field. Luna didn't wait to see if it was snagged before it hit the ground. She took off toward first base like a house afire. Angie liked to watch her run.

"Sure you don't know her?" Jack teased.

"Dad, leave it alone."

"Can't help it, pumpkin. An old man has a right to want to see his one and only daughter happy."

It was a speech he'd given her before. She didn't understand it then, and she didn't understand it now. It's not like she was unhappy. "I'm happy, Dad."

"No, but you could be if you'd unwind a little."

Unwind? Like him? Focusing more on finding the happiness in the bottom of a water pipe than on raising her son? No, thanks, not for Angie. "I'm wound just fine."

"Angie—"

"I'm fine," Angie said firmly. She was done with the conversation. It was useless to discuss something that simply would not change. Angie was determined not to take her focus away from Oliver, and

Luna looked too good in leather to be interested in playing house. And she couldn't forget Luna's possessive girlfriend, who made it clear she didn't plan to share.

Angie tried not to watch Luna for the rest of the game, but couldn't help but notice when the game ended and Luna walked toward the parking lot with Ruby wrapped around her. They looked good together.

Angie was sure she and Luna would look better.

CHAPTER FOUR

Wednesday, July 29

Oliver dropped a staggering number of bags on the couch in a clump. Jack patted Oliver on the shoulder and went into the kitchen. If total packages were the meter used to judge a trip to the mall, theirs had been successful.

"You should see what Grandpa got me." Oliver's eyes were bright. Recently, he'd spent far too much time with a sullen pout on his face, and Angie was grateful for the change of attitude. She prayed it wasn't fleeting.

She sat in the vacant armchair next to the sofa. "Show me."

Oliver proudly displayed his treasures—a DVD, a video game, one pair of already torn jeans, several T-shirts, and, oddly enough, a cookie recipe book. Angie had a mixed reaction to her father and son's shared shopping. One part of her—the mature, mommy part—was excited for her son. How nice that he had such a good time with his grandfather. The other part—the shallow, petty part—was jealous that Oliver had shared yet another moment with her father that Angie had never experienced. Jack had never taken Angie shopping at the mall, or anywhere else, when she was Oliver's age.

All her clothes when she was younger came either from Goodwill or the Methodist church. Her father didn't attend services there, yet the members somehow felt a strange obligation to clothe his child. When she got old enough to work, she did. After that she bought her own outfits. She spent many Saturday nights babysitting so she could afford the perfect outfit for the prom.

Prom. God, what a disaster. That's the night she finally said yes to Oliver's father. The first and last time. It was enough to confirm that she was far more interested in her best friend, Lisa, than in her boyfriend. Unfortunately—or fortunately, depending on how she looked at it— Oliver arrived the requisite nine months later. A lesbian teenage mom. As if her life wasn't complicated enough with an absentee mother and a father constantly searching for the perfect high. She'd been scrambling to make up for that one night ever since.

"Need help carrying all this to your room?"

Oliver kissed her cheek. "No, Mom, I got it."

Moments like that melted Angie a little. She loved the glimpses of the sweet boy he was before surly demons took over his personality. Perhaps he would eventually grow out of this Dr. Jekyll and Mr. Hyde stage.

Angie heard knocking at the kitchen door, then Tori called, "Yoo-hoo, anybody home?" For some reason Tori got a kick out of greeting them like a yokel, which always made Angie smile.

"In here."

Oliver scooped up his packages and headed toward his bedroom as Tori entered the room.

"What's that?"

"Massive loot from my trip to the mall with Grandpa," Oliver answered with a devious smile.

"Score." Tori bumped knuckles with him around his shopping bags before he retreated to his room and closed the door. She settled on the couch, her feet crossed at the ankle and resting on the coffee table.

That drove Angie nuts. "What are you doing here?"

"I'm happy to see you, too." Tori tried to glare, but still smiled.

"Get your feet off my table and then I'll be happy."

Tori left her feet where they were. "I want you to go somewhere with me."

"Where?" They had to be at work in two hours, so they didn't have much time for errands.

"Coraggio."

"Why?"

"Because you need to get laid and there's a certain tall, dark, and handsome tattoo artist there who would love to accommodate you."

Angie snorted. "Right."

"Whatever. You can let your vagina grow old alone. Don't say I didn't try to help."

"Did you actually need something?" To the outside observer, Angie might come across as bitchy. To Tori, she definitely came across that way, but that was part of the fun in their relationship. They expressed their mutual love by being snarky.

"Seriously, I want to have her check my tattoo. Thought we could stop on our way to work."

"Why there?" Angie was skeptical.

Tori looked at Angie like she was dense. "Because she's the one that did it."

Angie heard the silent *duh* at the end of Tori's sentence.

"Tori," Angie spoke slowly, "contrary to your opinion, I'm not looking to get laid. I'm perfectly content with my life as is." Angie could taste the subtle lie in her statement and didn't like the texture. She might not be looking for sex from just anyone, but that didn't mean she would say no if Luna offered.

"I just want to have her take a look, Angie." Tori met her gaze and held it. "Really."

"Okay."

"Besides, have you seen her apprentice? Gorgeous."

Suddenly Tori's persistent request made sense. "So this is really about *your* desire to get laid?"

❖

The real-estate listing promised abundant space, low rent, and a semi-decent neighborhood. The odds of getting stabbed in the parking lot were fairly slim, but Luna's car stereo system might not survive the move. Providing the place wasn't condemned when they viewed it in person, the location was perfect.

"This is the one?" Luna asked, but she knew the answer when Perez showed her the paper.

Perez nodded. "Yeah, I think so."

"Okay, call the agent."

Luna had found the current location for her business. All the difficulties in securing the right place made it that much more special. This was her home. Since opening Coraggio, Luna had grown more attached. Her sense of ownership was no longer linked directly to the building they were standing in, but rather to the very heart of the business. She wanted Perez to feel the same things she had. This was the first step.

Perez pumped her fist. "All right." She took the paper and headed toward the phone in the back room.

It was an overcast day, typical for Portland, even in July. Luna looked out at the gray sky barely visible between the building across the street and the top edge of her window. The weatherman promised more hot days. Luna hoped he was right. She wasn't ready for summer to be over.

Two women were huddled on the sidewalk outside her front door. Angie and Tori. Luna smiled at the realization. They appeared to be arguing, and Luna hurried over to let them in. She didn't flip on the neon *Open* sign as they didn't officially start business for another thirty minutes.

"Come on in." Her voice was rough even though she'd been up and talking to Perez for a few hours. Too many cigarettes in her twenties. She put as much flirtation into her smile as possible and directed her dimples full bore to Angie. Despite her reputation, it'd been a long time since she'd put effort into impressing a woman. She hoped she came across as sexy and charming, not desperate and trying too hard. The thought of not being cool made her falter temporarily. "Decide to get a tattoo after all?"

Angie gave her a small smile as she entered the showroom and brushed her hand over Luna's arms as she passed. "Hardly."

"Nope, she's afraid of hot women bearing needles," Tori quipped. "A fortune-teller at the state fair warned her against your kind last year."

Luna closed and locked the door behind them so no one else would wander in until they were ready to open. "What if the hot woman agrees to put away the needle in exchange for a completely different kind of penetration?" Luna usually made this kind of careless statement to Perez—off the cuff and humorous in a completely inappropriate kind of way. She regretted it immediately.

Angie's face flared red and she coughed. Tori patted her on the back and laughed. "Good, it hasn't been so long that you didn't get what she meant."

Angie coughed harder.

"I'm sorry." Luna felt like a jackass. She shouldn't be flirting with Angie in the first place. That was part of her agreement with Ruby. Not that she wouldn't flirt, but that she wouldn't take it further than that. Angie made her forget all about that promise. Any way she looked at it, she *was* a jackass.

"Let's try this again. What brings you here today?" Luna tried for professional courtesy, but her last comment had destroyed the distance required for that.

Tori tried to stop laughing, her face turning almost as red as Angie's from the effort. Luna was worried she'd have to perform mouth-to-mouth if she didn't get things under control soon. "Would you care for a glass of water or something?"

"No." Tori swallowed a giggle and hiccuped. "I just came by to have you check my tattoo." She pointed to her shoulder.

Perez picked that moment to reappear. "Okay, we have an appointment to meet with the realtor on Mon—" She looked up from the paper she was reading and noticed Angie and Tori. Or, more specifically, Tori. Grinning, she said, "I didn't realize you were here. What's going on?"

"Need a checkup." Tori batted her eyes and Luna was impressed. She'd never seen another woman besides Ruby pull that off. Ruby prided herself on being able to snare a woman with just a look, and Tori obviously shared that skill, as Perez was drooling all over herself.

"Absolutely." Perez led Tori to the workshop area.

Luna was unsure what to do with Angie. Technically, she should be inspecting her own work. As it was, however, she was willing to leave it to Perez. She snuck several sideways glances at Angie. Each time they made eye contact, Angie looked away quickly, her ears still red.

"Wow, this is awkward, huh?" Luna figured the sooner they got through the uncomfortable beginning, the quicker they'd get to the getting-to-know-you middle stage. And she wanted to get to know Angie far more than she was comfortable admitting.

Angie nodded. "I'll just wait outside."

"The weather is crap. Stay in here and I'll leave you alone." That was a bit of a stretch. Yes, it was overcast and a bit gloomy, but the temperature was holding at just under 70 degrees, it wasn't windy, and, so far, not a single raindrop had fallen. A little cool for late July, but perfect by Northwest standards.

"I don't really want to be left alone." Angie's muttered response was so quiet Luna wondered if she was hearing things. She didn't push Angie to repeat it, but she took advantage of the opening.

"Why don't we just sit? I'm sure they won't be long." Luna led Angie to the rich brown leather couch. She used to be so confident when it came to women, but it had apparently been too long. She had no idea what to say or how to proceed with Angie.

Not that it mattered. She had Ruby. It wasn't love, but it was honest. She had to keep reminding herself that.

Angie fidgeted with her shirtsleeve and shifted from foot to foot. She glanced at the couch to Tori to the window. Her gaze settled on Luna. "I guess that would be okay." She sat.

Luna studied Angie. Her cheerleader-blond hair was swept up in a loose bun on the back of her head, tendrils drifting loose and framing her face. Ocean-deep blue eyes full of resolve and just a hint of fun, like maybe she remembered how to have a good time, but hadn't cut loose in a while. Pure speculation, Luna realized, but she couldn't stop drawing conclusions about the little things she saw in Angie, like the perfect tan that didn't make sense in a city known for its liquid sunshine. Did tan lines go with the out-of-place bronzed skin? How many layers of clothing would she have to remove to find them?

She edged closer to Angie and brushed the back of her fingers across her cheek. Her fingers barely skimmed the surface, but Luna felt their contact all the way to her toes. Every cell in her body was aware of Angie.

Angie closed her eyes and a shiver rippled across her skin. Luna was mesmerized. Luna inched closer, her lips so close to Angie's. The thought of kissing Angie became the center of her universe. She was ready to sacrifice everything to make it happen.

Angie's eyes flew open and Luna froze, her body on fire. She wanted so badly to chase those lips as Angie eased away from her.

"So, what is this?" She gestured between them.

Luna opted for denial. "What? We're just sitting here."

"You know what I'm talking about." Angie's direct approach was seriously sexy to Luna. Add the stern mommy voice and several naughty role plays ran through her mind.

Luna knew *exactly* what Angie was talking about but wasn't willing to admit it. "No, I don't." She hoped Angie would drop it.

Angie looked at her like she was the idiot child in a long line of idiots. "The flirting, the innuendo, the damn charge every time we're within two feet of one another. I'm not imagining it."

"Oh, that." What else could she say?

"You have a girlfriend."

That's right, Angie had seen her with Ruby twice now. "Sort of."

"Sort of?" Angie snorted. "What exactly would Ruby be if not your girlfriend?"

"It's complicated." Luna tried to think of a way to explain Ruby that wouldn't make her sound cheap and easy. "But she's not my girlfriend."

"So what is she?"

This was not a conversation she had envisioned having with Angie—ever. Yet here she was trying to think of the right way to say she and Ruby were fuck buddies. "Our relationship is based on mutual agreement and need."

"That's the arrangement I have with my hairdresser, but I don't French *her* in the middle of a ball field."

"We have sex, but that's all." Luna was shell-shocked. She never felt the need to justify her relationship. She was an adult, dammit. If she wanted to fuck someone, that was her business, nobody else's.

"Are you exclusive?"

Luna nodded. This was not going well.

"For how long?"

"Three years." The answer made Luna cringe internally, but she refused to show it on her face.

"That's not complicated. She's your girlfriend."

Luna didn't argue. She sat there, silent and defeated.

"Where do I fit into that?" Angie's voice lost some of its confidence. She sounded much younger than she had a moment ago. Luna wanted to comfort her.

"I don't know."

Whether Angie would acknowledge it or not, it *was* complicated. Regardless of her relationship with Ruby, Luna was drawn to Angie. She wanted more.

"Then you have to stop." Angie nodded firmly. "*We* have to stop."

Luna agreed. Angie's assessment of the situation amazed her. Technically, they hadn't *done* anything. Most women would cling to that fantasy and ignore the obvious signs. They wouldn't be brave enough to vocalize their thoughts as Angie had.

Angie left her sitting there, with torrents of Angie and Ruby spinning in her head. As Angie exited Coraggio with Tori in tow, Luna landed on one concrete truth. Despite their need to stop, or perhaps because of it, Luna wanted Angie more than ever.

CHAPTER FIVE

Wednesday, August 12

The grocery store was definitely a personal hell for Luna. Every time she went in search of something simple, the trip morphed into a major outing. All she wanted was a gallon of chocolate milk and a steak for tonight's dinner. First was a battle for the only open parking space—which Luna won, but she did have a slight pang of guilt for forcing the other driver to the overflow parking lot. Then the dairy cooler was completely empty. Yes, they explained about the cooler malfunction, and no, it wasn't anybody's fault. But damn she had a craving and all the excuses in the world wouldn't make it go away.

Finally, she saw Angie, like some sort of sexy apparition, standing in the meat department. Should she say hello? Or should she just duck and be done with it?

But Angie looked so good in her faded jeans and worn T-shirt, trying to pick out the perfect roast. Luna resisted as long as she could, then succumbed to the magnetic pull. She strolled casually to where Angie stood.

"Hi, Angie."

Angie smiled briefly, then her eyes hardened. "What are you doing here?" She said it like she *owned* the store. The attitude simultaneously pissed Luna off and turned her on. She squirmed; moisture and leather were a horrible mix.

"Came in for a steak." Luna noticed a boy next to Angie and wondered how long he'd been there. Probably the entire time. She was a little single-minded when it came to Angie.

"Hi, you must be Angie's son." Unsure how to greet a child, she extended her hand like she would with an adult. He took it with a smile.

"I am. Who are you?"

"Right, sorry. I'm Luna. A friend of your mom's." Were they friends? She doubted Angie thought so, but hoped she'd let her get away with saying it.

While she was introducing herself, Tori joined them, her smile much more genuine than Angie's. She bumped hips with Angie and placed a bottle of red wine in the top of the shopping cart. Luna was jealous of their casual intimacy, but grateful that the gestures held no sexual vibe. They were obviously friends only.

"Luna? What a coincidence." The way she emphasized *coincidence* made Luna suspicious. Perez, after all, was responsible for the outing to the grocery store as well as the one to The Cadillac. She pictured Tori and Perez laughing as they plotted to bring her and Angie together. She felt manipulated.

"I'm Oliver," Angie's son interjected, unwilling to be pushed aside as the adults moved on with the conversation. "I like your tattoo."

"Thanks." She'd gotten the angel on her right bicep on the first anniversary of her mother's death. The grief that everyone told her would lessen had stayed with her, hard and unrelenting in the pit of her stomach. It swarmed up and engulfed her at the least likely moments. The angel she'd chosen in tribute to her mother shocked those who knew Angela Rinaldi. Rather than a soft, flowing design, Luna had chosen a hard-lined relief image. The tattoo lacked angelic details, but conveyed strength and certainty.

"Did it hurt?" Oliver asked with youthful exuberance, and Luna hoped Angie didn't blame her for his enthusiasm.

Before she could defer the question, Tori chimed in. "Yeah, did it?"

"A great deal." The answer surprised Luna, since the actual tattoo had been little more than irritating. The pain behind it had been crippling.

"Oh." Their simultaneous response made Luna smile. Disappointment looked the same regardless of age.

"It was nice seeing you, Luna." The look on Angie's face didn't agree with her statement. "But we need to get back to our shopping."

She started to move away and Luna panicked. When would she see Angie again? "Wait." She placed a hand on Angie's arm. It was a light touch, but the power of the contact jolted her. "I want to see you again." Luna cringed. Instead of cool and smooth, her mouth opted for bumbling and forceful. Again.

Angie looked at her far longer than was comfortable and Luna squirmed. Still she couldn't stop her mouth from charging forward without her brain. Later, when she had a moment to think, she would likely regret her lack of control. Angie left her defenseless, and she wasn't sure yet if that was a good or a bad thing.

"Let me take you out. I know Saturdays aren't good, but surely you have a night off. I could take you to dinner or a movie or—" Luna clamped her lips shut, aborting her stream of babble, and waited.

"Oliver, get a loaf of bread," Angie said, her voice level.

"But—"

"Now, son."

"Okay, fine." Oliver inched his way toward the bakery section.

"Tori?"

"Hmmm?"

"Go with Oliver?"

"Not a chance. No way am I missing this. It's better than daytime television."

Luna suddenly wished she could accompany Oliver on his quest for baked goods. That would certainly be more fun than whatever Angie had in store for her. The woman did not look happy. Luna squared her mental shoulders and waited.

"What are you doing here, Luna?" The question held a lot more judgment than it did the first time Angie asked it.

"Getting steak, I told you." Luna smiled, then remembered that her charm didn't seem to work on Angie. "I came over to say hi when I saw you because I didn't want to be rude."

Angie didn't look convinced. "And what was that? Just then? With the dinner invitation in front of my son. You do not get to bring him into this."

"I'm sorry. You were leaving and I couldn't just let you go."

"Luna, you're not being fair. I told you, I'm not comfortable with this…this…whatever *this* is. You have a girlfriend."

"She's right, you do." Tori's contribution was not helpful. Luna ignored her.

"What do you want, Angie? You want me to break up with Ruby?" When the words left her mouth, Luna felt overwhelmed. The truth in the question left her breathless and lightheaded. The thought of losing what she shared with Ruby was surprisingly easy to accept. But the fact that she was willing to do so for a woman she barely knew, a woman who acted like she didn't want to know her, was emotionally murky. She wasn't ready for the very real feelings that fueled her attraction to Angie. Until that very moment, she'd been able to lay it off as lust. Now she had to confront her intentions. She clutched the side of Angie's cart like it was a life preserver.

Tori squeaked and clapped. Angie's expression, however, did not change. "Would you?"

"Yes." The simplicity of the answer furthered Luna's shock. It also strengthened her resolve. She didn't know what was happening inside her, but her mother would be disappointed if she didn't have the courage to find out.

"You don't even know me." Angie's statement, blunt and to the point, made Luna cringe.

"I want to." God, what was it about Angie that made Luna abandon all reason? She was going along great, then she met Angie and wham! Sharp left on illogical street. All her emotional self-preservation instincts abandoned her at the same time.

"Why?"

"Let me show you." Luna struggled to control the situation. She'd already laid herself out for Angie, Tori, and every other person shopping in the meat department. She refused to give Angie an itemized list of why she was attracted to her, not with an audience. Besides, she wasn't sure she could vocalize her feelings in a concise, easily quantified manner. Emotions were sloppy.

Maybe it was the way Angie fidgeted and chewed her lip when she was nervous. Maybe it was the steeled confidence to say what she thought, to ask questions others would leave alone. Maybe the combination of sexy girl-next-door mixed with nurturing lady Madonna. Maybe the shy smile that made Luna want to protect Angie, even as she pushed her away. Maybe it was just Luna's relentless hormones driving her to chase the girl who said no. Maybe it was all that, along with a million other little things that Luna had yet to discover about Angie.

Angie's smile was small and a bit uncertain, but Luna felt victorious. She'd finally said the right thing.

"Now what?"

"A date." Feeling more confident than she had since she saw Angie across the aisle, Luna expanded on her intentions. "Have a little food, drink a little wine. Get to know one another." She took a half-step closer to Angie.

"Stop there." Angie took a matching half-step back.

"I'll stay three paces away from you at all times if that's what you want." It would kill her, but she'd do it. "But sometimes it's good to not think, isn't it?"

Oliver returned with the loaf of bread. "This the right one, Mom?" At Angie's nod, he tossed it into the cart. "Are you two done, or are you going to send me to get something else?"

"We're done."

Luna didn't agree, but didn't want to push her luck. Still, she had to ask one more question. She hesitated. Angie hadn't reacted well when she asked in front of Oliver before. She had to be careful. "When would you like…" She was proud of herself. The desperate clutching she felt in her chest at not cementing the date didn't make its way into the question. She sounded confident, even if she couldn't finish.

"I'm off on Monday."

"Should I call you to confirm?" It required a great deal of tact to ask for a phone number with Angie's son two steps away. In her club days, she'd simply say, "Hey, babe, can I have your number?" That wouldn't work with Angie.

"Sure." Angie scribbled it on the bottom of her grocery list. Before turning it over, she looked at it, shook her head once, then handed it to Luna. "I can't believe I'm doing this."

"Me either." Tori laughed. "But I love it." She high-fived Luna when she walked by.

Luna tucked the number in the back pocket of her leathers and slapped her hand against Tori's outstretched one.

Luna was halfway home before she realized she'd forgotten the steak.

Thursday, August 13

Angie tried to focus on her textbook, but her thoughts kept looping back to Luna and their last meeting. And, more important, their next meeting. Of course, if Jack and Tori would give it a rest she might be able to silence the nagging voice in the back of her head that kept asking what the hell she was thinking.

"You should have seen her, Jack." Tori munched on a carrot stick, using it like a baton for periodic punctuation as she spoke. "Standing in front of the meat counter in her leather pants. And she pulled it off. I could never make leather work, let alone at ten a.m. in the middle of the grocery store. She's totally hot."

Angie glanced at Oliver to make sure he was engrossed in his video game and not their conversation. It was bad enough that he had witnessed part of her exchange with Luna; he didn't need to hear Tori dissect her potential love life.

"Leather, you say?" Jack stood at the stove stirring a batch of fudge. He was the only person Angie knew who gave in to the craving regardless of the season.

"Yeah, dark brown, not black. Super sexy. You'd want to date her."

Ack! Angie had been trying to deny that little nugget, the reason she'd resisted Luna so thoroughly. Jack *would* want to date Luna, and that left an uncomfortable, squishy feeling in Angie's stomach. She forgot all about it when face-to-face with Luna. Hell, she could forget—or possibly find—anything in those eyes. But sitting in her kitchen, confronted by her father's history of dating, she couldn't ignore it. Angie did *not* want to date any of her father's women.

"I have my hands full at the moment."

"I mean where do you even *find* pants like that?" Tori asked. "Leathers-R-Us?"

"No." Jack poured the candy into a pan to cool and wiped his hands on his apron. "There's a great place on Lombard."

Jack's current girlfriend—and every one that came before her—likely shopped at the same stores as Luna.

"Oh, for God's sake. Can you two talk about something else?" Why the hell had she said yes to Luna? She was not Angie's type, so why, when she meant to say *no*, did *yes* come out of her mouth?

"We could, but where's the fun in that?" Jack asked.

Angie lifted her book higher, effectively blocking her view of her father.

"And she had this long brown hair with this sort of wild, loose curl thing going on," Tori said.

"What kind of brown?" Jack had always been big on details.

Tori dipped a finger into the fudge clinging to the edge of the pot. "Kinda like fudge, actually. It's all dark and rich." She popped the finger into her mouth. "God, that's good."

"That right?" Jack poured the candy into a pan and offered the spoon to Angie. He ate it himself when she declined. "She have rich, dark hair, Angie?"

"Yes, Dad, she wears sexy leather pants and has wild dark hair."

Angie's outburst was lost on her father, and he continued like she'd never commented. "Wait a minute, is this the same woman you were staring at during Oliver's ball game?"

Crap, that was not a set of dots she wanted her father to connect. "Yes."

Tori asked, "She was at Oli's game? Which one?"

"No, she was at her own game. It just happened to be at the same park."

Tori made another pass at the fudge. "I miss one game and see what happens."

"I *knew* it." Jack sat at the kitchen table and pushed a chair out for Tori. She settled in next to him, and they faced each other like two housewives ready to gossip about the neighbors. "Angie denied it, but I could tell there was something between them two."

"How come you didn't let me know?" Tori batted at Angie's arm. "Did you guys talk?"

Angie glared at Tori, then returned her attention to her textbook without answering.

"No." Jack took up the conversational slack. "They just kept staring at one another. I've been around. I know when someone is being cruised."

That her father even knew the term *cruised* made Angie squirm, especially when he used it regarding her.

"You should see the two of them together. The heat they put off is amazing."

Jack beamed. "Tori's right. She's hot."

"She's a lesbian, Dad. You can't have her." The irony over her almost-perfect quote of Ruby didn't escape Angie. Was Ruby's grasp on Luna as imperfect, nonexistent, even, as Angie's? Apparently so, since Luna was ready to throw Ruby over the second Angie showed even the tiniest amount of willingness. Yet another reason to not get involved with Luna.

"No, but she's perfect for you." Jack's simple endorsement made Angie want to run.

"I'm going to study in the living room." Angie closed her book and left the kitchen.

The more her father voiced his approval of Luna, even though it was based on nothing more than appearance, the less sure Angie was about her decision to go out with her. But it was too late to back out now.

Friday, August 14

Luna finished inking a cartoonish rocket circling Saturn. Perez peered over her shoulder. "Looks good."

"Mmm." Luna's brain was bouncing between the grocery store where she'd run into Angie two days ago and the conversation she needed to have with Ruby in a few minutes. The tattoo she'd been working on distracted her in the moment, but when the soothing buzz of the gun stopped, her mind raced off again.

"You plan to add anything else?" Perez asked.

Luna spun the barber chair so the occupant could see the design in the mirror. "What do you think, Stacey?"

"Perfect." The rocket was Stacey's latest addition to the space opera canvassing her back and upper shoulders. Luna was proud of her work.

After Stacey paid and ushered her girlfriend outside, Perez asked, "Have you figured out what to say to her?"

"No." Luna never should have told Perez what she had semi-promised Angie. She still hadn't figured out how to approach Ruby, but she needed to do it soon. If she didn't talk to Ruby by the time she picked Angie up for their date on Monday, there definitely wouldn't be a second.

"Well, you have about fifteen seconds, because here she comes." Perez gestured toward the small BMW parked along the curb. Ruby was crossing the street.

"Great." Luna didn't have another appointment scheduled for two hours.

"You're doing the right thing." Perez escaped into the back room as Ruby slithered in the front door.

The endorsement from Perez didn't mean much. She'd never liked Ruby.

"Hello, lover." After her customary greeting Ruby stepped in close for a kiss.

Luna stepped back. "We need to talk." That was not what she meant to say. Nothing good ever started with that phrase. She'd put Ruby on the defensive before she even determined exactly where to take the conversation next.

"Well, that doesn't sound good." Ruby evaluated Luna levelly. "Should we go upstairs?"

"No." Luna didn't want to be alone with Ruby and a bed. She was weak. Then again, Ruby deserved a little privacy. Perez would be an unforgiving audience at best. "Yes." She shook her head. "I don't know."

Ruby took Luna's hand and led her up the steps. "Come on."

Luna followed, her thoughts circling inside her, but never settling on one concrete idea.

"So?" Ruby stood with her hands on her hips. Even though it was Luna's apartment, she looked like she owned the place. "What did you want to tell me?"

Luna debated sitting on the couch but decided against it. She'd face Ruby head-on, standing on her feet. "I met someone."

"I meet people all the time. What's your point?" Ruby tapped her foot and her temple twitched.

"She's different." Luna was not saying this well.

"Luna, I have exactly," she checked her watch, "forty-seven minutes until my nail appointment. I planned to spend that time naked and you are really fucking that up. Say what you need to say."

Luna took a fortifying breath. "I want to date her."

"So date her. What does that have to do with me?" Ruby started to undo the buttons on her blouse but Luna placed her hand over Ruby's, stilling her motion.

Her whole relationship with Ruby slammed into sharp relief. Despite their sex-only approach, Luna had been confident in their commitment. They'd both promised not to sleep with anyone else while seeing each other. Ruby's casual dismissal made her wonder why Ruby was so willing to overlook Luna dating someone else. Did she really think this was the next evolution in their relationship, rather than the end of it?

"I can't see both of you."

"Why in the world not?" Ruby's voice was hard, but her chin trembled slightly.

Luna pushed her hands through her hair and pictured Angie. Was she out of her mind for even considering giving up a woman like Ruby? Ruby had the softest skin in the history of skin, and God, the things she could do with her hands. Luna had no real idea what Angie had to offer, but she needed to find out. Soft skin and hands aside, Angie compelled her. Luna could not ignore the burning for Angie.

"She wouldn't like it."

"So that's it, then? Three years and it's over because you *met* someone?"

Luna could feel a tantrum building and wanted to duck for cover. She stood her ground.

"Ruby, we both knew this would end eventually." Luna had always assumed Ruby would be the one to leave.

"No, Luna, *we* didn't know that." A fat tear clung to Ruby's eyelashes for a moment, then streaked down her face. "One of us thought the other would eventually figure it out. I waited for three fucking years for you to pull your head out of your ass and get a clue. For nothing." Ruby's voice increased in volume and pitch as she gained steam. Her rant ended in a near screech.

Luna didn't know what to say. "I'm sorry."

"Sorry?" Ruby's voice was a bit calmer, but still on the edge. "Fuck off, Luna." She slammed out of the apartment, leaving Luna in her wake.

CHAPTER SIX

Monday, August 17

Tori gestured for Angie to spin in yet another circle. "That's what you've decided to wear?"

Angie abruptly stopped. All the spinning was making her dizzy, and there was absolutely nothing wrong with her outfit. "Yes. It's fine."

Tori nodded, but her expression said she didn't agree. "What if she takes you somewhere *nice*?"

"We live in Portland. There are only two or three places where jeans and a blouse wouldn't be good enough." Portland was the land of Tevas and dreadlocks. Even in the dead of winter, shorts—combined with thermals on top—were commonplace. Wearing long jeans in the summer was considered dressing up. "Besides, she said to dress casual."

"Don't you want to impress her?" Tori bordered on whiny.

"What do you think I should wear?"

Tori bounced to the closet and pulled out a light summer dress. "This," she said victoriously.

"You realize Luna will probably wear leather pants. Is a dress really the right complement?" Angie let herself dwell on that thought for a moment. Luna in her born-to-be-bad leather outfit and her in her girl-next-door skirt. It was a nice visual. "Okay, dress it is."

"Yes!" Tori tugged at Angie's shirt with such fervor Angie almost forgot why her best friend was trying to get her naked.

"I can do it." She wrenched the fabric away from Tori in fear that she'd pop the buttons off completely.

"You have to put your hair up." Tori moved on to her next point of attack before Angie could finish changing.

"I'll make you leave if you don't settle down." Angie dropped her pants and stepped out of them.

"No, you can*not* wear that underwear." Tori looked horrified.

Angie regarded herself in the mirror. It'd been so long since she'd gone on a date she'd completely overlooked her lingerie. Last year's boy-cut briefs and industrial bra really weren't sexy. Tori dug through her underwear drawer and re-emerged a moment later waving a matching dark blue set like a victory banner.

"Put these on."

"Bossy much?" For all her grumbling, Angie was grateful for Tori's presence. Tori dated. She thought about things like shaving her legs and wearing the right panties.

Underwear changed, Angie squirmed as the string part of the G-string settled in her ass crack. No wonder this had been lost at the back of the drawer. The bra wasn't any better. The underwire, while doing a fabulous job keeping her breasts pointed the right direction, was also digging into her left boob like a small animal furrowing out a place to sleep for the night. She wiggled, trying to find a comfortable position—but no. The underwire was determined.

"You look good." Tori's eyes were glazed and her voice breathier than normal.

Angie knew Tori didn't want *her*. Tits and ass turned her on no matter who they were attached to. Once she pointed out a nun with a wink and a nudge. All Angie saw was habit and piousness. "Knock it off. I don't have time for your lust-filled thoughts. Tell me how to keep this from poking me."

Tori blinked. "You don't."

Angie gave it one last tug and resigned herself to a night of wanting out of her clothes. "At least it distracts me from the permanent wedgie my panties are giving me."

Angie slipped the dress over her head and stepped into the shoes Tori handed her. Tori then spent twenty minutes worrying Angie's hair into a loose pile on the back of her head. Angie could have achieved the same look in thirty seconds, but she didn't tell Tori that.

"Looks nice." Tori fingered the loose strands hanging at the side of her face. "Now, makeup."

The reflective moment over, Tori brusquely applied it to Angie's face with the careful efficiency of a professional.

Angie felt like a French whore and wanted to scrub her face. Her skin couldn't breathe. "Are you sure I need all this?"

"Stop complaining." Tori spun her around to face the mirror. "Look."

"Wow." It'd been too long since Angie had taken this much time. She'd forgotten about the wonders of Maybelline. "I look beautiful."

"Sweetie, you always look beautiful." Tori squeezed Angie's shoulders. "Tonight you look like a movie star."

They stared for a few moments too long and Angie had a flash of panic. She'd overdone it. Luna had specified casual. She looked anything but casual.

"It's too much."

"No, it's perfect. Leave it alone."

The doorbell rang as Angie reached for a washcloth.

"She's here." Angie's stomach fell. Eventually she'd have to figure out where it landed and put it back.

"Yes, so stop fussing and go answer the door." Tori pushed her out of the bathroom and toward the front door.

Oliver and Jack waited in the living room, looking a bit too happy. Tori stood next to them and they all smiled ridiculously big at her. "Go on," Tori made a shooing motion, "answer it."

Angie took a deep breath and turned the knob to find Luna grinning and thrusting out a bouquet of daisies. Beautiful and simple. They were perfect for a first date.

"You're here." She sniffed the flowers and cursed herself for sounding like an idiot.

"I am." Luna looked around Angie into the house, but Angie didn't invite her inside. She didn't want to listen to anymore teasing from her family about Luna, now or in the future.

Without looking, Angie held the flowers out behind her and asked,

"Tori, will you put these in water for me?" When the flowers left her hand, she stepped out the front door and called out her good-byes over her shoulder.

Luna held the gate open and ushered Angie onto the public sidewalk. There was no car—or motorcycle—in sight. "It's a beautiful night. I thought you'd enjoy the walk."

Angie wasn't sure what to do with her hands. If she left them at her side, would she accidentally brush against Luna? Would that be so bad? The dress didn't have pockets, so that was out, and crossing her arms felt...wrong. Luna took Angie's hand, effectively ending the internal debate. Angie savored the feel of Luna's palm flush against hers—a perfect fit.

"Mmm." Angie breathed in the cool evening air. "Where are we going?"

"Well," Luna hesitated, "I didn't want to take you to a restaurant since you spend so much time in one already. And a movie, while a fun way to pass the time, would get in the way of our actually talking, and that's the whole point, right? Talking, getting to know each other."

Luna's avoidance made Angie suspicious. "Okay," she stretched the word out, making it last longer than its short four-letters worth, "but *where* are we going?"

"My place," Luna blurted. "I cooked dinner for you."

Angie didn't respond immediately. Her brain was too busy rolling around the implications in Luna's statement, trying to decide how she felt about it.

"We can do something else if you want. It's nothing fancy, very portable. We can have a picnic at the park, or—"

Angie squeezed Luna's hand. "I think it's lovely."

"I think *you're* lovely." Luna sounded like a star-struck teenager.

"Thank you." Angie blushed.

Rather than the leather pants Angie expected, Luna wore a pair of soft denim jeans with a broad studded belt. A chocolate-brown men's button-down tucked in at the waist completed the look. The top two buttons were open. When Luna moved just right, Angie could see the hint of a tank top underneath.

Luna murmured her thanks and they walked in silence for a few blocks. It wasn't as awkward as Angie anticipated—first dates were always nerve-wracking, and she hadn't been on one in so long that first-date jitters had grown outrageously in her memory. This felt different from what she expected. She was almost comfortable. Well, as comfortable as she could be with the constant surge of energy that ran between her and Luna.

"I forgot to say thank you for the flowers. That was very thoughtful."

"I'm glad you liked them." Luna led them through a narrow alleyway that ran alongside Coraggio. The path led to a small courtyard with a solitary set of stairs, which she ascended, still holding Angie's hand, then unlocked the door. "Here we are." Luna stood to the side and let Angie take in the scene.

Luna's home was small, but meticulously cleaned and organized. The kitchen table, covered with a long bone-white linen tablecloth, was topped with full place settings, white taper candles, and an open bottle of Chianti left to breathe before dinner. Luna produced a lighter and set flame to the candles.

"I hope you like lasagna. It's one of the only things I can cook with any kind of consistent results."

"Sounds good." Angie had eaten very little all day because of her nervousness about her first official date in months. The delicious smells wafting out of Luna's kitchen brought her hunger back full force.

Luna poured Angie a glass of wine. "I just need to warm the bread. You can wait in the living room if you'd like, pick some music perhaps?"

Angie took a small sip of wine. She preferred to stay and watch Luna cook, but she nodded and went in search of Luna's CD collection. Along with the expected rock, Luna had a few surprises. Angie selected her favorite Al Green and swayed with the music as she returned to Luna.

"Great choice." Luna popped a Kalamata olive into her mouth. "Want an olive?"

"Sure." Angie reached for the bowl, which Luna quickly pulled away.

"Let me." Luna held the small fruit to Angie's lips, the juice dripping from her fingers. Angie opened her mouth, closed her eyes, and extended her tongue. She took it delicately from Luna, and the slight contact as Luna's fingers brushed against her tongue thrilled her. She savored the eroticism of the moment, along with the rich, meaty olive. When she opened her eyes, Luna was staring at her, her eyes dark and intense.

"You are going to make the three-foot rule very difficult, aren't you?" It was barely a whisper.

Angie turned away and gulped a mouthful of wine. "Is dinner almost ready?"

"Almost." Luna set the dangerous bowl of olives on the table next to a small tray of Caprese. Angie loved the simple salad of mozzarella, basil, and tomato.

"Can I help?"

Luna put a bowl of bread on the table next to the lasagna and said, "No, that's everything." She held out Angie's chair for her and waited for her to be seated. With Angie snuggled up close to the table, Luna placed her hands on Angie's shoulders and spoke into her ear. "I really hope you like this."

Angie shivered. Luna's hot breath against her ear and glancing off her neck made her want to turn her head and capture Luna's lips in a kiss. She remembered the way they felt barely there against her own. That aborted, nonexistent kiss had melted Angie. The memory of it stayed with her, taunting her with how good the real thing would feel. Would it match her imagination?

Angie barely managed to answer. "Looks good."

Luna lingered for a few moments longer, her lips close to, but not touching, Angie's skin. Angie held her breath, caught in Luna's steady inhale and exhale. Luna's hands eased away from Angie's shoulders, her fingertips brushing the bare skin of her upper arm, and she stepped away. Angie forced air into her lungs.

"Here," Luna cut a portion of lasagna, "let me serve you." She dished it on to Angie's plate, along with some Caprese.

After she filled her own plate, Luna sat opposite Angie. Thank God. Her close proximity was driving Angie nuts.

Angie took a bite of the lasagna. "Delicious." She closed her eyes and savored the flavor. It was better than Jack's, not a small feat. "Who taught you to cook?"

Luna scratched her bicep and hesitated before answering. "My mom."

"Yeah? Are the two of you close?" Angie took another bite.

"Yes, we were." Luna tucked into her salad, avoiding eye contact.

Already Angie regretted asking that. The answer was obviously making Luna uncomfortable. Still, she continued. "Were?"

Luna stopped eating and placed her fork carefully next to her plate. "She died several years ago."

"Oh." Angie had no idea what to say. Everything that came to mind sounded like an empty platitude. She settled on a simple "I'm sorry."

"It's okay." Luna shrugged and resumed eating. "What about your mom?"

Suddenly it was Angie's turn to be uncomfortable. "She's around somewhere, I'm sure."

Luna took a couple more bites, then said, "We should find a happier topic, like...the weather. It's been really nice." She offered a weak smile.

Angie laughed, but felt strained. "Yes, this weekend was gorgeous. Did you have a game?" Angie felt a twinge as she remembered her only sighting of Luna at the ballpark—a pleasant memory until Ruby had teetered in with her heels and swept Luna away.

"No, I hardly ever play."

"Really? You did very well when I saw you."

"Thanks, but I usually opt to sleep on Saturday morning."

Angie broke off a bite of bread that had been brushed with olive oil and garlic. "Then why did you play that day?"

"Because I knew you'd be there."

The candlelight was the perfect complement to the red flush in Angie's cheeks. Luna wished she had a hundred more comments just like that one if only to watch Angie blush.

"You came to see me?" Angie's blush deepened.

Luna nodded and took a sip of wine.

"So why did you bring Ruby?"

Luna's calm ruptured again. Why didn't she see that coming? She traced the conversation, took a larger sip of wine, and said, "I didn't. Her showing up interrupted my plan to talk to you."

"You didn't look terribly disappointed."

She'd set the trap for herself. She could have avoided the ballpark, let herself be patient, and talked to Angie the next time she passed in front of her shop, but she couldn't do it. She just had to see her, and of course Ruby just had to show up. Luna mustered a defense. She wasn't committed to Angie, she shouldn't have to explain. "I'm sorry."

Angie folded her napkin, set it on the table, and looked Luna in the eye. "We never did finish this conversation the other day, did we?"

"Which conversation?" Luna wanted to sit quietly and enjoy Angie, not talk about Ruby.

"The one about you and Ruby. And me."

And there it was, all laid out and impossible for Luna to ignore.

"Do you think there is a you and me?" Luna placed more importance on Angie's answer than she wanted to admit.

Angie leaned in slightly. "You said you planned to talk to Ruby. Did you?"

"Yes."

"And?"

"And I told her I can't see her anymore and that's that." Luna simplified the story for Angie. In truth, her last meeting with Ruby had been horrible.

"She was okay with that?" Angie asked.

"No," Ruby's reaction still shocked Luna, "but what choice does she have?"

Angie resumed eating, but she kept her eyes on Luna. "That depends. What choice did you give her?"

"None." Luna was done avoiding the subject. If Angie wanted to know what she was willing to give up at her request, Luna would damn well tell her. "I told her I wanted to date you and couldn't see her at the same time. You wouldn't allow it."

Angie's features relaxed. She swirled her wine, the deep red catching in the flickering light. "You told her that?"

"It's true, isn't it?"

"Yes, but I don't have the right to make that kind of demand."

"I know." Luna would have liked to give her that right, and the immediacy of the thought frightened her. She barely knew Angie, but couldn't wait to discover every bit there was to learn.

Angie seemed willing to share a comfortable quiet moment, and she took another bite of lasagna. They had a lot to reflect on.

"Luna." Angie took a deep breath. "I'm not sure how this will go, or why you're willing to let me demand so much, so soon."

Luna opened her mouth to respond, but stopped when Angie held up her hand.

"Oliver is my whole world, and I don't know how you'll fit. But I want to try."

Luna set her fork carefully on the edge of her plate. This was an important conversation. She didn't want to be distracted by food. "Me, too."

"You may change your mind." Angie smiled, but still managed to look sad.

Luna shifted closer and debated taking Angie's hand. She didn't. "Let's find out."

"I don't know what it is about you. You're not my type."

"What is your type?" The answer mattered to Luna.

Angie fingered the edge of her napkin. "It's been a long time since I've thought about that." She spoke quietly, hesitantly. "I want a woman who loves completely, thoroughly, and forever. I want to fall asleep and wake up in her arms. I want a woman who will dance in the backyard without any music, climb under the sink to fix the drain, and sit in the bleachers and cheer for Oliver whether he hits a home run or strikes out. I want a woman who isn't afraid to giggle during sex, who makes me feel…everything." Angie took a sip of wine. "And I want that woman to let me give her all those things in return."

The air around them was heavy and hot. Luna loosed the cuffs and rolled up her sleeves. She wanted to take off her top shirt completely, let some cool air reach her skin. "That's what you want?"

Angie met her gaze and nodded. "Yes."

"Then I'm exactly your type."

"Mmm." Angie returned her focus to her lasagna without further comment.

When they finished the meal, Luna wanted to ask Angie to stay. She wanted to ease that flowing skirt up around her waist and explore for hours. Instead she led her to the door. "Let me walk you home."

"Don't be silly. I'll be fine."

Luna started to protest. She wanted to extend her time with Angie even if it was just for the brief walk. Before she could fully form her argument, Angie stepped into Luna's personal space and palmed Luna's cheek. "Tonight was wonderful." She kissed Luna gently, and Luna became lost in the glide of Angie's lips against hers.

"When can I see you again?" Luna asked, her face inches from Angie's, breathing her in.

"Soon."

Luna kissed her again, letting herself go a little longer. She pulled Angie tight against her, amazed at the perfect fit of their bodies. "Tomorrow?"

"I can't, I have work." Angie spoke with their mouths still joined.

"Before work?"

"I'll try." Angie pulled herself away, and Luna focused on calming her breathing.

Luna kissed Angie one last time before she slipped out the door. She needed to be patient. "Try hard."

She watched Angie until she was out of sight, certain that *soon* wouldn't be soon enough.

Chapter Seven

Wednesday, August 19

The Cadillac was uncharacteristically busy for a Wednesday night, and Angie ran to keep up with her diners' demands. The service might be irreverent, but that didn't mean they were sloppy or inattentive. An empty water glass was the kiss of death for a tip. God knew Angie needed her tips.

"Angie, want to split the twelve-top with me?" Tori spun through the kitchen door with an arm full of empty plates and quickly entered three orders into the computer system.

"Absolutely." Angie handed Tori a tray loaded with food, slid another onto her shoulder, and led the way back onto the floor.

Tori dodged a rambunctious businessman who had knotted his tie around his head like a bandana. "You still haven't told me about your date."

Technically, Angie hadn't had time to talk to Tori. Tuesday Tori had spent the day in Seattle with her mom, and tonight hadn't been conducive to conversation.

Angie offered the condensed version. "It was nice."

"Nice? Nice ain't gonna cut it."

They arrived at Angie's table, so all Tori got in response was Angie's silent brow raise. They served the diners, refilled glasses and bread bowls, made a few inappropriate comments, and were off to Tori's new table of twelve.

Angie picked up the conversation on the way. "Okay, it was *really* nice."

"You need to start confessing." Tori left the "or else" off the end of her sentence, but Angie heard it loud and clear.

Angie smiled at Tori and circled to the opposite end of the table as Tori gave her spiel welcoming the diners to The Cadillac. They bantered and played with the group of semi-reserved women, trying to draw them out. It was rare that a group of only women dined here, and Angie preferred to fend off grabby men than engage reticent women. She knew exactly where she stood with the louder of the two sexes. And they tipped better. With women, she was always unsure where her tip would land. If she was ever in doubt with men, she could undo another button on her shirt, but that simply didn't work with women. Okay, not *all* women.

"Do you like working here?" A young blonde looked over the top of her glasses at Angie. It seemed silly to Angie. Why wear the glasses if you didn't need them?

"It pays the bills." Angie shrugged. "Do you like where you work?"

The blonde ignored Angie's question and asked another. "Even when men try to grab you like that?"

Angie tried to remember someone trying to touch her in the last few minutes. She came up blank, but it happened often enough. Dodging hands was second nature for her now. "It's not that big of a deal. Are you ready to order or should I come back in a few minutes?"

"But do you like it?"

Wow, she was a pushy woman. Angie seriously considered telling her to get fucked, but before the words could slip out, Tori came to her rescue.

"She's a lesbian, honey, what do you think?" Tori asked, and Angie was grateful for half a second until Tori kept speaking. "A lesbian who goes on dates with hot tattoo artists and then doesn't tell her best friend how they went."

The table stopped talking and looked at Angie and Tori.

"Could we not do this now?" Angie offered Tori a saccharine smile. "I'm sure these women are ready to order."

"No, this is interesting." The blonde made a keep-going gesture. "We'll wait until you're done."

Christ, Angie did not want to have this conversation like this. "It was *one* date, not dates, with *one* tattoo artist. And I told you, it was nice." She started to leave.

"Nice? Well, that doesn't say anything at all, does it?" another woman at the table speculated.

"No, I didn't think so either," Tori said.

"I will get you for this." Angie chewed off each word. Tori was officially on her list.

"I don't doubt it." Tori smiled a little too big and Angie shook her head. Her friend was truly irritating at times.

"We had dinner at her place. She fixed lasagna."

Yet another woman chimed in. "Ooh, she cooked? I love it when they do that."

A fourth woman giggled. "Did she light candles? Candlelight has the strangest effect on my clothes. They just fall right off. It's the damnedest thing."

"What about music?"

Tori high-fived the two women who spoke up. "Good questions." She crossed her arms and looked at Angie. "Well?"

"Yes, there were candles. No, they didn't make my clothes fall off. And we listened to Al Green." She didn't point out that she had selected the music. She wanted the inquisition to be over as quickly as possible. "Now, who wants to eat?"

As the women ordered, Angie's nerves calmed. She was still unsure how she felt about her date with Luna. She didn't want to have an affair with no hope of real commitment, and even though Luna seemed to offer more, was she capable of keeping that kind of promise?

They finished up, and as Angie made the rounds at her own tables she pondered the first woman's question. Did she like working at The Cadillac? Angie did what she needed to take care of Oliver. Work was a means to an end. She needed money; this is how she earned it. In truth, she would like to do a hundred other things for work instead of wait tables, but until she finished her degree years from now, she couldn't even think about it.

"Angie," her boss bellowed from near the front door. "Delivery for you. Make it quick."

A young man stood next to her boss, eclipsed almost entirely by a bouquet of white calla lilies. They were beautiful.

By the time she reached the front, her boss had signed for the delivery and stood reading the attached card. "Who the hell is Luna?"

Tori squealed from somewhere behind Angie. "She sent you flowers?"

Angie claimed the card and flowers and carried them to the back. This added one more ring to the circus the night had been already. The card read *Is it soon yet?* and was signed with Luna's name and phone number. Angie tucked the card into her pocket.

"They're gorgeous." Tori reached around Angie and smoothed her finger over one of the flowers. "Did you sleep with her?"

Angie sputtered. "What the hell kind of question is that?"

"A legitimate one. I'm curious." Tori shrugged.

"You really think I'll tell you anything else after that little stunt out there?"

"Come on, Angie, that was a harmless bit of fun. They loved it."

Tori had laid her bare to work a tip. Amazing.

"I didn't." She tried to pass Tori, who wouldn't budge.

"I'm sorry, won't happen again."

Tori was incorrigible, but that was part of her charm. Angie loved her in spite of it. "Okay."

"So," the devious glint was back in Tori's eyes, "did you have sex with her?"

"No."

"No?" Tori's face scrunched up. "Why not? There was candlelight, good food, some seriously sexy soul music. Don't tell me you said no."

"I definitely didn't." Angie was as perplexed as Tori. She'd been trying to figure out why their date had ended as it had. If she hadn't been foolish enough to bring up Ruby, they surely would have had sex. The mood was set. All they had to do was take advantage of it, yet they hadn't.

"You wanted to?"

"Of course I did." Angie worried that Tori might be losing it completely. "Have you *looked* at Luna? She's hot, remember?"

"I do remember. I also remember that you told her no when she asked you out. You had to be persuaded. For all I know, that same rule applies to your thighs. Maybe you need to work up to letting them open." Tori moved to the servers' station. It was time to get back to work.

Angie trayed up her next order and mumbled, "They were plenty willing to open."

"Then why on earth didn't you guys do it?"

"I don't know." Angie remembered Luna's demeanor from that evening. After her admission about breaking up with Ruby, Luna seemed to hold back. Finally, Angie had given in and kissed Luna instead of waiting for her to make a move. It had been wonderful and over far too soon.

"You planning to call her?" Tori asked over her shoulder as she exited the kitchen.

Angie followed.

Would she call Luna? "Maybe."

Friday, August 21

The mound of paperwork was back on Luna's counter and it had grown. She had thought that sifting through the real-estate listings would reduce the looming pile of paper. Instead it seemed for every one she removed, three more magically appeared.

"So what do we put in this box?" Luna tapped the section marked Income with her pencil eraser. They agreed it was a bad idea to use ink until they knew exactly what they wanted to write. At this rate, pencil didn't seem to be working out any better. She had erased so many times the lines on the form were blurred and fading fast. "Do they want to know my income from tattooing? Or the expected income from the other artists, too? Should I include the rent I'll get from this building?"

"I don't know." Perez tugged at her short hair. She looked almost as frustrated as Luna felt.

The overhead bell rang and Luna looked up, glad for the

distraction. It was too late to do another tattoo, but they could still schedule work if a client wanted.

Angie and Tori entered, Tori eating an ice cream cone, Angie a frozen yogurt. It was the first time Luna had seen Angie since their date, and her heart pounded.

"What are you working on?" Angie offered Luna a spoonful of her dessert, and Luna lowered her head and opened her mouth. Angie's pupils dilated as she placed the plastic spoon between Luna's lips. Her gaze remained focused on Luna's mouth long after she'd finished the bite.

Luna cleared her throat, choking on the heaviness. "Nothing." Her voice was rougher than expected. She collected her papers and handed them to Perez without glancing in her direction. She didn't want her good thoughts about Angie being corrupted by the brain-cramp-inducing loan application.

"So we're not interrupting?" Angie stopped walking just short of Luna's personal space and offered Luna another bite of her yogurt.

All Luna could do was shake her head no. No to the interruption and no to the yogurt. She kissed Angie on the cheek, a polite, chaste greeting, when she really wanted to explore her lips. They were warm and inviting last time. What would they feel like cold and tasting of vanilla?

"Thank you for the flowers." Angie spoke while her mouth was close to Luna's ear, and her cool breath tickled Luna's skin. Luna held her breath as Angie continued. "They're beautiful."

"I'm glad you liked them." Luna fought to clear her head. She'd sent them for a reason. "Does this mean you'll see me again?"

"I'm seeing you right now."

Thank God Perez was entertaining Tori. She was not up to playing hostess. All she could focus on was Angie's perfect, deep, deep blue eyes. Like the ocean, they invited her to swim in them for days, lost and not looking for land. The desire made her dizzy. She needed desperately to sit. "Come with me." She tugged Angie toward the couch.

"Wait," Angie resisted, "I need to use the restroom first." Even though it was a statement, Angie's inflection made it feel like a question. Luna found it irresistibly cute.

It took Luna a moment to realize Angie didn't know where the bathroom on this level was, thus the question mark at the end. She recovered her senses long enough to give Angie directions.

Perez and Tori were already sprawled on the couch, so Luna sat at the table instead. She had a cup of coffee from earlier and automatically took a sip. It was room temperature and tasted like old socks. She set the drink on the table and waited for Angie to return.

"Do you have plans on Labor Day?" Tori was playing with Perez's hair, and Luna felt like a voyeur. "Noonish?"

"What's going on?" Perez slid a little closer, her hand moving to Tori's thigh.

Luna stood. She couldn't sit and watch them, but Tori's next words piqued her interest. "There's a barbecue at Angie's house. I want you to come."

The rest of their words faded away. Maybe that's why Angie had dropped by, to invite Luna to her family get-together. The holiday was several weeks away, but the possibilities excited Luna.

Luna switched off the neon *Open* sign and threw the bolt on the door. She was on autopilot, focused more on thoughts of Angie in shorts and a spaghetti-strap tank top sipping iced tea and eating a burger than on closing her shop for the night. Luna took the money from the cash box and locked it in the safe. She'd worry about the paperwork tomorrow when Angie wasn't there.

"We're getting out of here." Perez had her arm possessively around Tori's waist, her fingers hooked in the top of her jeans.

"You can make it home without me, right, Angie?" Tori asked. Angie had returned without Luna realizing.

She smiled at Luna. "I'll be just fine."

They left and Luna locked the door behind them. When she turned around, Angie was standing very close. She tilted her head up, and her eyes fluttered shut. It was a classic kiss-me pose and Luna's head swam again. What was it about this woman that affected her so thoroughly?

Angie's lips parted and her tongue darted out briefly. The shining wetness lured Luna closer, ever closer, until her mouth was against Angie's, just the whisper of their lips touching. She could feel Angie's breath against her skin more firmly than the pressure of her lips.

"I missed you." Angie whimpered and pulled Luna closer, her fingers threading through the short hair at the base of Luna's neck. Their lips pressed together fully and Luna smoothed her tongue between Angie's teeth. She needed to taste…everything. Angie was a delicacy that Luna intended to savor.

Before Luna was ready, Angie withdrew. She stood, forehead against Angie's, watching her, memorizing the details. Angie wore a lazy half smile, her lips swollen and glistening. Her eyes were closed, and her breath puffed on Luna's skin, erratic and warm. Her fingers played through Luna's hair, tugging and pulling, alternating between soft caress and stinging tug.

It was perfect.

"Upstairs." Angie nipped at Luna's bottom lip. "Now."

Uncomfortable in the role of aggressor, but desperate for *something* to happen, Angie sucked on Luna's cherry-red lip—swollen from Angie's lack of patience—and soothed it with her tongue. If Luna didn't lead her up those steps soon, Angie would strip her bare and splay her against the plate-glass window for the greater Portland area to see. It'd been too long and she was done waiting.

She worked Luna's shirt loose and rested her hands on her waist, relishing the electric charge when she touched Luna's naked skin. The shock roused Luna and she backed slowly toward the stairs, stumbling when her heels hit the bottom step.

Luna groaned and pulled Angie's hands away. "You have to stop touching me if you want to make it to my bed."

Angie struggled out of Luna's grip, unwilling to suffer even a moment without feeling Luna's smooth body. The loss was too sharp. "Who said anything about a bed?" Angie popped open the pearl snaps that stood between her and more of that searing flesh. Luna stood on the step above her, a goddess in the halo of light from the room above. Angie covered her abdomen in wet, open-mouthed kisses, teasing the tense muscles with sharp little nips as she slid the shirt from her shoulders. "I just want you naked and beneath me."

She nudged Luna's legs apart and forced herself onto the same step. Luna struggled to stay upright, then fell back, landing on the stairs behind her with an *oompf*. Luna's eyes were round and Angie loved the control she surrendered to her with that look. Angie draped herself over Luna, driving her thigh between her legs. Luna shivered and pulled Angie to her, her mouth hot and demanding against Angie's throat.

Luna's teeth scraped against her pulse point, then she sucked hard enough that Angie knew she'd need a turtleneck the next day. Her stomach clenched and the thrill tumbled in a hot wave through her body. "Oh, God." Angie should have known that Luna wouldn't let their relative positions force her into a passive role. She was the kind of woman who could top from the bottom.

Every pent-up frustration. Every tightly controlled emotion. Every time she'd said no when she really wanted to say yes. Angie let it all go as Luna thrust her hips upward, causing the thick denim seam of her jeans to scrape roughly across her clit. Her body quaked and her eyes rolled back into her head.

"No!" Luna growled, and flipped Angie over, her back hitting the rigid rise of the stairs hard enough to leave a bruise. "You do *not* get to come before I even touch you."

Luna stripped Angie's shirt and bra before she had a chance to fully recover her breath, her fingers frantic and greedy. She palmed Angie's breasts, alternating between rough kneading and gentle caresses. Angie gripped Luna, her hands wrapped around her wrists, torn between guiding her lower and holding her hands to her chest. "More."

Luna rolled her nipples—thick and erect—squeezing them between her thumbs and forefingers. A jolt shot from Angie's nipples to her clit and she bucked her hips. Just a little more. She was oh-my-God close.

The touch ended as it started, without warning and before Angie was prepared for it. Luna stood, running her hands over Angie's body in a fleeting caress as she pulled away. She stared at Angie, her eyes heavy and dark, her chest heaving as she removed her own bra, followed by her other clothing. Naked, Luna stood before her. No other tattoos, Angie thought absently as Luna bent over her.

"This isn't how I wanted to do this." Luna held herself just out of Angie's reach as she undid the snap and zipper on Angie's jeans. She tugged them off, but avoided touching Angie's skin—a touch Angie desperately craved. "I would have taken you in my bed, with candles lit, soft music playing."

"You can still do that." Angie sat up, reaching for Luna. She was throbbing for release, and however Luna wanted to do this was fine so long as she did it *now*.

Luna caught Angie's hands and brought them together. Holding them tight in one hand, she stretched them over Angie's head, still keeping herself close enough to *feel,* but not close enough to touch. She straddled Angie's body, forcing her prone with her weight.

The sensation of full-body skin-on-skin contact, combined with the wet slick of Luna open and ready against her abdomen and the sound of her voice saying deliciously naughty things in her ear, stole Angie's focus. Black dots crept into the periphery of her vision as she arched into Luna, prolonging their contact.

"I would have fucked you hard wearing a strap-on cock." Luna left a hot trail of arousal over Angie's stomach. It matched the fire burning its way through Angie's belly to her clenching vaginal walls. "But only after I'd made you come with my tongue and sucked every last drop of excitement from you."

"God," Angie gasped. The throbbing crested, nearing full crescendo.

Luna raised up, moving between Angie's thighs and forcing them wide. "Bend your knees for me, baby," she urged, her voice a soft counterpoint to the porn-like narrative she'd been engaged in. Angie complied and Luna went back to her low, rough monologue. She shifted her hold on Angie's hands, strengthening her grip as she used that arm to keep her weight suspended over Angie. "But you wanted to do this here." She worked her other hand down, down, down between their bodies, staring hard into Angie's eyes. One finger gently nudged Angie's clit, a fleeting touch, and Angie twitched and thrust wildly. God, she wanted those fingers on her. In her.

The fingers—Luna's godlike, heavenly fingers—returned, stretching her lips wide, leaving her clit exposed and vulnerable. The cool air prickled against the sensitive skin for a second, then Luna was against her, their clits burning together in a soaring, wet symphony.

Luna trembled above her, her eyes holding Angie's for a moment, then slammed shut as they ground their hips together.

Tension pooled in her belly, gripping and building as she thrust against Luna, lost to everything but the slick glide of Luna's clit against her. Luna released her hands and gripped the stair on either side of Angie's head, pulling sharply on Angie's hair. With her hands finally free, Angie scratched lines across Luna's ass, clenching and releasing only to repeat the desperate grasp with every roll of Luna's hips. She forced Luna against her in a frenetic, escalating rhythm.

Luna grunted. "God, you feel so *fucking* good." She snapped her hips hard against Angie and moaned loud and long, her body shuddering and arching.

All the coiling tension in Angie's body drew tighter, then sprang apart, shattering her from the inside out. She pulled Luna to her, wrapping her legs and arms around her, desperate for the solid weight of her body to keep her from coming completely undone. Luna's mouth covered hers, her tongue thick and invading, swallowing Angie's voice as she climaxed.

They lay together, gasping and sweat-covered. Luna smoothed Angie's hair and kissed her softly, licking along her bottom lip. "I think I like your way of doing this better."

Angie tried to sit up, only to flop back, her muscles limp. "I don't think I can move."

Luna pulled her closer. "I'm just fine right here."

"For now." Angie brushed a chaste kiss on Luna's forehead, eyes, and finally her lips. "Eventually, though, you have to make good on your promises."

"Definitely."

Tomorrow Angie would be sore, bruised, and in desperate need of a hot bath. Tonight, however, she was grateful for a few stolen minutes when she could forget about being the perfect mom and focus on just feeling good.

She sighed. Just like that, one fleeting thought about Oliver, and the moment was over. Angie needed to get home. She forced herself into a sitting position, and her body protested loudly.

"What's wrong?" Luna squeezed her shoulder.

"I need to go." She pulled on her clothes and flipped her hair out of her collar. It was a total wreck.

"Stay with me?" Luna's eyes said so much more about wanting to hold her than those three words.

"I can't." Angie found her shoes and put them on, wanting to explain about her son, about how he would never know if she spent the night away, not if she got home early enough, but *she* would know. That was enough to get her on her feet and walking out the door. "Oliver."

Luna nodded and escorted her to the door, slipping on her shirt and pants as she walked. "I can give you a ride."

"No, that's okay." Tonight, more than any other, Angie needed the time to cool off before she arrived home. "I'll walk."

"When can I see you again?" Luna asked as she held the door open.

"I don't know." Angie kissed Luna one last time, the earlier heat missing from her awkward, shuffling good-bye on her way out the door. "I'll call you."

Angie walked away feeling like a grade-A jerk. Instead of saying, "Yes, I'd love to see you again," she'd turned an erotic, fun encounter into a booty call.

Jerk.

CHAPTER EIGHT

Monday, August 31

Angie moved her blue game token forward two spaces and took another card. She needed a twelve to win the game. She drew Sorry—a great card if you were still at the beginning of the game, but with three game pieces already home and the fourth solidly on its way, the game's namesake card was simply annoying. She groaned. "Your turn, Oli."

She loved nights like this, when she didn't work and Oliver was in the mood to indulge her love of board games, especially Sorry. Lately he'd claimed it was for babies. She'd tried logic, pointing out that she loved it and she was too old to be a baby. He was not convinced.

Oliver drew an eleven and laughed maniacally. He split the count between two game pieces, knocking one of Jack's pieces, as well as Angie's remaining piece, back to Start. Murphy's Law told Angie she wouldn't draw another Sorry card until the game was over. She groaned again.

"Why did I agree to play this with you?" she asked Oliver as Jack completed his move.

"It was your idea." Oliver gave her a toothy smile, far too happy to be defeating them. He took a bite of his pizza and gestured for her to go.

"What's your rush?" Angie postponed the inevitably wasted move. She hated having her only player sitting at Start. It was like the penalty box of Sorry.

"Just draw your card." Jack had three men still at home, with no reprieve in sight. Losing made him grumpy.

Angie drew a twelve and discarded it, disgusted with the irony.

Oliver won on the next move and Jack conceded. Just as well. Angie had no enthusiasm for competing for second place. It seemed a silly standard to strive for.

"Congratulations, son."

Oliver grinned like a fool, despite his initial protests about being too old to play.

They boxed up the game but remained at the table, eating the takeout pizza Jack had supplied for dinner.

"So, Angie." Jack spoke far too carefully, which made Angie nervous. "You've been seeing a lot of Luna lately."

Angie felt guilty. She'd timed her visits with Luna to coincide with Oliver's activity schedule because she wasn't willing to sacrifice her time with him. It never occurred to her that her father would miss her.

"Yeah, Mom. You should have her over for dinner so we can all get to know her." Oliver's contribution sounded rehearsed, and Jack subtly nodded.

Angie shook her head. "I don't think so."

"Why not, Angie?" Jack asked. "I've never even met her. I'd like to know who my daughter is spending all her time with."

Jack's sentiments didn't impress Angie. Too little, too late for her to take it to heart. When she was younger he never showed the slightest interest in her dates. In her mind, he'd forfeited the right to exercise parental concerns. She was twenty-seven years old, for Christ's sake. She didn't need Daddy's approval of her beau.

"It's not a good idea." As much as Angie enjoyed Luna, she didn't want to expose Oliver to a temporary person in her life. She had no doubt that her relationship with Luna would be short-lived, so why approach it any differently? Women like Luna simply didn't settle down, and unlike Jack, Angie didn't intend to parade an endless line of leather-clad women before Oliver. Not that she'd dated any other women like Luna, and she certainly didn't plan to turn it into a habit.

"Why not? You obviously like the woman. Would it be so bad

for your son and your old man to get to know her?" Jack spread his hands—like he was laying it all out for her—and smiled.

"I've never brought anyone home to meet Oliver."

"No, but you should." Jack's smile faded slightly.

Angie collected the game and stood. It needed to be put away, and she needed an out from their conversation. She met and held her father's gaze, debating whether she should tell him how much she resented all the women he had brought home when she was young. She hated meeting all her new "aunts." Finally, she shook her head once, then left the room.

"Angie, you'll have to unlock that heart of yours eventually," Jack called to her back. "Not all women are out to hurt you."

"Don't be silly, Dad." Angie raised her voice to be heard from the living room. She returned to the kitchen but didn't sit.

"If you two intend to argue, I'm out of here." Oliver stuffed the remainder of his pizza into his mouth and left. Music came on in his room, this time at an acceptable level.

"Are we arguing?" She didn't agree with Jack's version of her needs, but she was almost certain they weren't just discussing it.

Jack ignored her question. Maybe he thought they were. "What are you afraid of?"

"Dad, I'm not having this conversation. I don't plan to bring Luna into our home. If you're having difficulty with the time I spend with her, I can cut down. I don't need to see her every day." And she didn't. She could probably survive forty-eight hours without seeing Luna, but the thought of testing the theory made her stomach clench.

"And that's it? You won't even talk to me about this?"

"There's nothing to talk about." Angie shrugged. She still hadn't relinquished her post in the open door. She rested her shoulder against the frame and crossed her arms over her chest. She'd read somewhere that crossed arms, or arms held in front of the body, said she wasn't engaged, that she wanted the conversation to end. Jack must not have read that article because he just kept pushing.

"Yes, there is. You've been to see that woman every day for the last two and a half weeks. Your family wants to meet her."

"Oliver has met her." Angie was still trying to figure a way to mentally unring that bell. She didn't want him to have the image of his mom dating a woman who wore leather pants and tattooed people for a living. Fortunately, Luna didn't wear the leather often. Angie preferred her in jeans. Or out of jeans.

"I haven't," Jack said quietly, "but I'd like to."

"No, Dad. I promised myself a long time ago that I wouldn't introduce Oliver to anyone I was seeing unless I was sure she was the *one*. If it were up to me, Oliver wouldn't have met her that day at the grocery store. I won't bring her here for him to get attached to. Absolutely not." Angie said more than she intended. She didn't have to justify her decision to Jack, even if he was her father.

Jack threw his arms in the air, a classic I-give-up gesture, and spun around to the sink. He attacked the dishes with extreme vigor.

Angie left the room.

Friday, September 4

Luna ran her fingers over Angie's back, starting at her shoulders, swirling and teasing to the dip just above her ass. Everything about Luna in the afterglow surprised Angie. She'd expected the leather attitude to carry over into all aspects of Luna's personality, including postcoital snuggle time. The first time Luna curled herself around Angie, she had been too stunned to fully appreciate the intimate move. Now she basked. Luna made her feel worshipped.

"Feel good?" Luna asked lazily as she lightly scratched her way up to Angie's shoulders.

"Mmm-hmm." Angie rested her head on her folded arms and closed her eyes. She loved the way Luna touched her.

"Tell me something." Luna's hands traveled farther this time, kneading Angie's ass cheeks. Squeeze and release, squeeze and release. She drew her fingers to Angie's neck and started the journey downward again.

"What?" Angie would tell Luna anything, including her checking account number and PIN, just to keep her magical hands moving over her body.

"I don't know. Something. Anything." Luna followed her hands with her lips. "I just want to know you."

Luna's kisses sparked against her, pleasure blooming outward from the touch of her lips, distracting Angie. "Be specific. I can't think when you do that."

"Tell me about your mom." Luna slapped Angie once on her bottom, sharp and quick, then urged her to turn over.

Angie settled onto her back and looked into Luna's eyes. Luna resumed her careful exploration along the plains of Angie's abdomen and into the valley between her breasts.

What could she possibly say about her mother? A woman who didn't love her enough to stay. "My mom didn't want to be a mom. She left when I was five."

Luna kissed her tenderly. "I'm sorry."

Angie shrugged and closed her eyes. She loved her time with Luna, without the pressure of work and parenting. She could relax, escape, and talk about secrets she otherwise held close to her chest. "I remember her packing all her clothes into a giant red suitcase. It probably wasn't that big, but when you're little, everything is huge. Then she took me to the neighbor's house, Mrs. Castanetta, and told me to stay there until my father got home. She kissed my cheek, patted my hair, and that's the last time I saw her."

Luna continued her massage, spreading goose bumps across Angie's chest and arms. Her nipples puckered.

"Were you scared?"

"No." Angie remembered standing at the kitchen counter with Mrs. Castanetta, a tall wooden stool under Angie so she could reach as they mixed cookie dough. She let Angie eat the first one. "My dad didn't figure out where I was until the next afternoon. I thought he'd gone with my mom."

Luna's fingers stilled. "He didn't know where you were that whole time?"

"There were large chunks of my childhood when he didn't know where *he* was. Losing track of another person when he was in that state? Not that big of a stretch."

Luna nodded and pressed a small kiss to Angie's temple. Her

breasts brushed against Angie's arm. "Where did your mom go?" Luna asked.

"She could be living in Gresham for all I know." The thought of her mom living in the nearby suburb left a bitter aftertaste in Angie's mouth. She thought she'd let go years ago. Apparently not. "Or Tibet."

"Do you have any good memories of her?"

"She had a beautiful smile." Angie could picture her mom's face, frozen forever in memory as she scooped Angie into her arms and said, "That's my Angie girl. I love you, baby."

"So do you." Luna caressed Angie's lips, her middle finger dipping inside to touch Angie's tongue.

"Tell me about your mom?" Angie knew Luna would likely change the subject. She always did. "Please."

"Angie." Luna closed her eyes and sorted out her words before answering. Her mother had been everything to Luna, but no matter how she tried to explain that, it always came out sounding less. Her mother deserved a tribute that Luna couldn't provide. Angie made her want to try. "She was my best friend, and when she died a part of me went with her."

Angie urged Luna to lie next to her, and she snuggled in close, her arm and leg thrown over Angie's middle and her head resting on her shoulder.

"Go on." Angie stroked her hair.

"Even though she'd been sick for so long, I didn't want to admit she was gone. I locked myself in my room with a bottle of grappa and almost missed the funeral." Luna's Uncle Frankie had found her and sorted her out, pouring cup after cup of coffee into her. And when he told her to have courage, sounding so much like her mother with their shared accent, she finally broke down and cried.

"Be brave, she'd tell me. '*Coraggio*, Luna, you must be strong.'" Luna didn't try to stop the tears that always came when she thought of Angela Rinaldi dying in that sterile hospital bed. She trusted Angie with her sadness.

"That's where you got the name, Coraggio." Angie ran her fingers through Luna's hair over and over, soothing Luna with the rhythmic motion. "What does it mean?"

"Courage." Luna tilted her head up and kissed along Angie's jaw bone. Kisses of thank you, not passion. She couldn't remember having a lover who listened, really *listened*. "She was so worried about me, about what I would do when she was gone."

In retrospect, Luna realized her mother had been right to be worried. Luna had not fared well after she passed. She surrendered herself into a cloudy drunkenness, surfacing briefly for the burial ceremony, then diving under again. She'd stayed obliviously numb for months until Uncle Frankie told her to stop disgracing her mother's memory and *do* something with herself.

And so she had. Luna had built a business to honor her mother, and now she was on the brink of dismantling that tribute and moving it to a different location. Would the heart of Coraggio remain the same, or would Angela Rinaldi's defining presence remain behind with the building? Luna told herself that her mother's spirit was in her, twined into her soul, not attached to the four walls of a structure her mother had never visited. Still, the fear, however small, was there, gnawing at Luna. She needed to change the subject before malaise settled over her completely. She was with Angie, and that was cause for celebration, not remorse.

"What was her name?" Angie asked.

Luna stroked Angie's hair, the soft strands gliding through her fingers. "Angela." The word was harder to say than Luna expected. It'd been too long since she'd said her mom's name aloud. And it had never mattered so much. She was trusting Angie with a part of her life that was sacred.

Angie didn't respond immediately. Her gaze softened, searching Luna's eyes. "We have the same name."

"I know." Luna blinked back a tear. "Change of subject." She propped herself up and kissed Angie on the mouth. "What are you doing this weekend?" Labor Day was the following Monday and Angie still hadn't mentioned the barbecue. Luna was beginning to get anxious.

Angie pushed herself away from Luna and moved to the edge of the bed, where she sat with her back to Luna and shrugged. "Not much." Angie stood and left the bedroom. "You want a glass of water?" she asked on her way to the kitchen.

That answered Luna's question conclusively. Angie hadn't mentioned the barbecue because she didn't intend to invite her. What did that say about their relationship? They had yet to go out. Yes, they'd had one date, but Luna had brought Angie back to her apartment. She'd thought fixing her dinner would be romantic, but since then their encounters were limited to Luna's bedroom and involved very few clothes and even less conversation. Their little bubble of existence was beautiful, but Luna wanted more.

Everything about Angie said she was a settle-down-and-raise-a-family kind of girl, yet she'd shown no signs of escalating their relationship beyond the physical. All the tumblers fell into place, and reality unlocked with a deafening click. She was Angie's dirty little secret. Normally Luna would find that wonderfully naughty. At that moment, though, she simply felt deflated. She'd thought they were building something together.

Luna got up and started to dress. She was tying her shoes when Angie returned.

She stood in the open door, sipping a glass of water. "Are you going somewhere?"

"I thought we could go get something to eat."

"Really?" Angie set the glass on the tall dresser and slinked toward Luna. The predatory gleam in her eyes and the sway of her hips almost melted the icy fragments that had settled into Luna's chest. Angie started unbuttoning Luna's shirt. "But it's so much better when you're naked."

Luna's resolve returned. She didn't want a repeat of her relationship with Ruby. If that was all she wanted, she wouldn't have traded one for another. Still, Angie looked so good standing before her, glistening skin and tousled hair. Luna wanted to fall to her knees and drive her tongue between Angie's legs. She loved watching her come from that angle, with Angie's hands in her hair, urging her closer as she fucked her hips into Luna's face. She'd taken Angie like that once, and when she finally climaxed, she'd collapsed on top of Luna.

She stilled Angie's hands, needing to know exactly what Angie thought of their relationship. She wouldn't be able to figure that out if she allowed herself to be distracted.

"You're not doing anything at all this weekend?" She gave Angie another chance to invite her into her life.

Angie stepped back and looked away. "Hanging out with my

family. Nothing exciting." Angie's gaze settled on her glass of water and she took a drink.

"Maybe we could do something. It would be nice to get to know Oliver." Luna felt like an asshole. A jealous asshole, but she couldn't let it go. "What do you say?"

Angie regarded Luna for a few moments, then crossed the room and pulled her work uniform from her bag and dressed hastily. "I forgot I promised my boss I'd go in early today."

"Sit with me for a minute?" Luna fought to keep the emotion out of her voice. Angie's obvious avoidance frustrated her. She caught Angie's hand as she headed toward the door.

Angie hesitated, then did as she asked. When Luna didn't speak, she said, "What?"

"Can we try this again?" Luna stroked her thumb over the back of Angie's hand. She couldn't thread together how they'd gone from naked and playful to dressed and serious so quickly.

Angie nodded, but her body remained tense. "I guess."

How could she ask what she wanted to know without sounding like an insecure jerk? Finally she just gave in to her curiosity. "I'd really like to get to know your family, Oliver especially."

"Why?"

Why? Why not? "Isn't that what couples do?" Wasn't it normal to want to be a part of her girlfriend's life? If, in fact, Angie considered herself Luna's girlfriend. Luna needed to clarify.

Angie shrugged. "I don't know. Is it required?"

Luna held Angie's hand carefully. Her past relationships had all centered on sex, but Angie looked like a stable, long-term-relationship girl. Luna's head spun, but that didn't keep her from asking Angie to explain. "Angie, what are we doing? You and I?" She paused to give Angie a chance to answer. She didn't, so Luna continued. "Are we just fucking? Because that's not enough for me. I want to be your girlfriend and take you on dates. I want to get to know your son and have him get to know me."

"Really, Luna? We've only been seeing each other for two weeks. That's too much." Angie rubbed her hands over her face.

"Three." Luna didn't know which was more disturbing, that Angie couldn't keep track of three weeks or that she thought it was too soon for greater involvement. Angie was willing to take her clothes off and spend hours rubbing their bodies together, but she wasn't willing to take her son to a movie together?

"Three what?"

"Three weeks, not two." Luna was dwelling on details to keep from thinking about the big picture.

"Okay, three. It's still too soon."

Luna tried again. "I'm not saying I want it all right now, but I would like to expand our relationship beyond this bedroom."

Angie didn't reply.

"Angie, please, this is important."

"Luna, this isn't about you." Angie stared at the bed. "Or me. I have to think about Oliver first." Angie's voice was flat, like she was negotiating an unwanted position.

"Let me help you." It was the best offer Luna could make. She hoped someone had offered to help her own mother when Luna was little.

"It's not that simple."

Luna wanted to hold Angie but knew she would get distracted. The conversation was too important for her to risk getting sidetracked. She kept her hands folded in her lap. "Talk to me."

Angie blew out a sigh. "He needs to know that he's the most important person in my life."

"Don't you think he does?" Luna brushed her fingers over Angie's arm. The need to comfort was too great to ignore.

"I hope so." Angie sounded far away. Luna wanted to tap into Angie's head and hear all the underlying reasons for her fears. As she was about to encourage her, Angie said, "After my mom left, my dad brought home a lot of women. Every single one of them had big hair, called me *honey*, and wore leather. I just wanted my dad to notice *me*, even once."

Luna finally gave in to her need and wrapped her arms around Angie. "I don't have big hair." She kissed Angie's eyelids. "I promise to never call Oliver *honey*." She kissed her nose. "And I'll throw out all my leather today. Right now, if you want."

"Tell me what you want." Angie tucked her head beneath Luna's chin.

"Invite me to your barbecue." Luna regretted her words immediately.

"I can't." Angie's body tensed and she pulled away from Luna. "It's just too soon."

Luna wanted to go to Angie's goddamned Labor Day barbecue, but was afraid she wouldn't win the battle. She didn't want a tense situation to escalate again. She compromised. "Okay, how about this? My friends are having a get-together next Sunday. Go with me?" Luna had known about the event for months, but had resigned herself to not attending when she and Ruby split. It was the perfect "safe" date with Angie. Not exactly public, but out of the house. The environment was friendly, and once committed, Angie wouldn't bail. Luna didn't know enough about her, but she was certain of that little detail.

"What's the occasion?"

"Their anniversary." Good. Angie was asking questions. She might actually go.

"What kind of gathering? Dinner? Party? Dinner party?"

"A low-key party." Luna was getting excited.

"Any chance I'll know anyone there?"

"Perez." Luna didn't want to mention Ruby. She weighed the cost of telling versus letting Angie discover for herself when they arrived. Full disclosure won over self-preservation. "Ruby will probably be there, too."

"I have to work." Angie's answer was firm.

"Can't you trade shifts with someone? Please?" Luna's request was out of character. Work came first. Suggesting that Angie request a last-minute schedule change showed how desperate she was. Angie's answer was more important than she wanted it to be. "Please."

"I could try." Angie didn't sound convinced. "And I'll have to make sure my dad can watch Oli."

Oli, not Oliver. How long would it be before she'd be comfortable using the nickname herself?

"Thank you." Luna kissed Angie's cheek. For the moment she was content to simply hold Angie's hand and trust her promise to try.

CHAPTER NINE

Labor Day, September 7

"Toss these on the grill for me, Angie." Jack handed her a platter of marinated steaks. This was their regular agreement for food prep. Jack did all the real cooking, but Angie managed to barbecue without destroying anything.

Oliver stood at the counter with Jack, trying to perfect the art of making a melon basket. Angie pilfered a chunk of watermelon and kissed the top of Oliver's head. Then she snatched a piece of ice from the bag in the sink and dropped it down the back of Oliver's shirt. He squealed and chased her to the deck. The steaks could wait until she'd thoroughly tormented him.

A couple of laps around the backyard and Angie surrendered. Oliver smiled sweetly, dumped a full cup of ice over her head, and ran inside before she could catch him. Could have been worse, she knew. Last time she provoked him, he'd doused her with the garden hose when she wasn't looking.

She loved days like this. It was eighty-two degrees, with a few fluffy, white clouds floating across the sky. Most important, Oliver was in a rare good mood. He could flip to surly at any moment, but hopefully his pleasant attitude would hold. She shook the last of the ice chips from her hair and collected the steaks from the kitchen. Giving Oliver a warning glare, she retreated to the deck.

"You need any help?" Tori entered through the side gate, holding a six-pack of beer. Angie was surprised to see Perez following close behind Tori, holding her other hand.

So that was how Luna knew about the barbecue this weekend. She felt like an even bigger jerk for not inviting Luna, but she just wasn't ready to set Oliver up like that. God forbid he got attached and then Luna disappeared from their lives.

"I'm good." Angie dropped the steaks on the hot grill one by one. The sizzling lulled her. "I'll take a beer, though."

Tori set the six-pack on the patio table, twisted the top off a bottle, and handed it to Angie. "Want these inside?"

Angie pointed to the red cooler next to the back door. "Cooler is full of ice. You can put them in there."

Perez opened two more, offered one to Tori and kept one for herself, then placed the remaining three in the cooler.

"Nice to see you, Perez." Angie hoped she sounded friendly. It wasn't Perez's fault that Tori invited her without mentioning it to Angie.

"You, too, Angie. Sure I can't help with anything?"

"Nope, I got this. You can check with my dad if you're dying to ball up melon. Personally, I think you should pull up a chair and relax." Angie took a sip of beer.

"I expected to see Luna here." Tori looked around the small backyard. An exaggerated, unnecessary motion since the entire yard was approximately the size of a cracker box. "Is she in the house?"

"She's not here." Angie flipped the steaks, closed the lid, then joined Perez at the table.

"Why not?" Tori looked genuinely confused.

"I didn't invite her." Angie forced herself not to fidget with the label on her beer. She didn't have any reason to feel guilty, so she had no reason to act like she was. Fidgeting, she'd read once, was a sign of guilt.

"Okay." Tori took a drink of beer and blessedly let the subject drop.

Sandy, Jack's girlfriend du jour, came through the back door carrying a bowl of potato salad. She set the dish on the table and took a beer from the cooler. How could anyone wear that much leather on such a warm day? The pants she understood as a safety precaution when riding, but the bustier? Angie couldn't come up with a single function it served other than sex appeal. Thinking about her dad and Sandy—and Sandy's reason for wearing sexy leather clothes around her dad—made Angie a little queasy. Luna would probably look hot as hell in the same outfit, but that didn't mean she wanted Oliver to see it.

"Sandy." Angie nodded toward her father's on-again girlfriend and flipped the steaks. "Where's my dad?" Sandy rarely ventured anywhere in the house without Jack at her side.

"Out front talking to Luna Rinaldi." Sandy didn't look happy about it.

"Who?" Angie choked. Sandy said Luna's name casually, like they were old friends. Figured.

Sandy took a long pull of her beer. "Luna Rinaldi. She did a couple of my tattoos."

Angie saw flames. No doubt Sandy was talking about her Luna. The same woman who Angie specifically didn't invite to their family barbecue. What the hell was she doing in her front yard, with Oliver in the kitchen with a front-row seat? She'd kill Luna. And Jack.

"I'm going to check on Oli." Angie headed toward the kitchen. "Tori, keep an eye on the steak?"

❖

Luna was fed up. The more she thought about the role Angie had relegated her to, the more upset she'd become. She needed to continue their conversation, to convince Angie that she could be the kind of partner that Angie deserved. But how could she do that? She didn't know what that kind of dedication looked like up close. She'd been raised by a single mom, and all her relationships had been spontaneous and short-lived. Until Ruby, that was. But how much had the three years they'd been exclusive counted since she hadn't made an emotional commitment?

She'd left Coraggio earlier with no destination in mind, letting her feet decide which way to go when she reached an intersection. Walking was therapy and Luna didn't get out often enough. When she looked up, she realized she was standing in front of Angie's house. However unintentional, she'd walked directly to the source of her frustration.

Laughter filtered out of the open door, followed by a squealed, "Mom, stop."

Then she heard Angie's laugh along with Oliver's. "What's the matter, son? You afraid of a little ice?"

Oliver laughed again, a desperate peal of giggles that made Luna smile. She pictured herself chasing Oliver and Angie around the kitchen and debated knocking on the door, but opted against it. No reason to upset Angie and humiliate herself by showing up uninvited.

She was about to leave when a motorcycle roared into the driveway and an older man, presumably Angie's father, walked out to meet it.

He ushered the rider, a woman he greeted with a lingering kiss, toward the house and was almost to the door when he saw Luna hovering on the edge of the yard. He sent his date in without him and greeted Luna.

"Hello," he said, with an inviting smile. His eyes reminded Luna of Angie's. "Are you coming inside?"

Crap, he thought Luna belonged there. She needed to extract herself as quickly as possible.

When she didn't answer right away, he continued. "You're Luna, right? Angie's friend."

"Yes," Luna shook his hand, "it's good to meet you."

"I'm Jack, her father."

He had a firm handshake, one that said he could be trusted. The look in his eyes as he regarded Luna said he loved his family and would protect them. Luna liked him immediately.

"So, what are you waiting for?" Jack gestured toward the house. "Good food and better beer are right this way."

Luna held back. "No, I really need to be going."

"Don't be silly. Angie is right inside. I'm sure she'd like to see you."

Luna wasn't sure of that. Angie had made it clear that she didn't want Luna to be a part of her family get-together. "I don't know—"

"And Oliver is looking forward to getting to know you. He hasn't stopped talking about you since he met you at the grocery store. Your tattoo left quite the impression."

So Angie had discussed Luna with her family and still didn't want her to come around?

"Perhaps another time." She took a hesitating step away from Jack, but before she could make a full retreat, Oliver burst through the front door. He ran up to Luna, almost tackling her. "Luna! You're here. Mom said you weren't coming." His smile was huge.

"I'm not. I was just walking by."

"You have to come in." He tugged on her arm. "You should see all the food. Me and grandpa have been cooking all morning."

As Oliver towed Luna toward the house, Luna stared at her feet, unable to believe they were moving. She certainly hadn't given them permission to do so.

"Oliver, wait." Luna planted her feet. "I'm not supposed to be here."

"Why not?" Oliver's eyes were big and brown, and when he looked at Luna, she wondered how Angie ever denied him anything.

Luna stuffed her hands in her back pockets and looked back and forth between Oliver and Jack. "I wasn't invited."

"What?" Oliver yelled, and Luna flinched. She never should have come here. Damn feet.

"It's okay, I'll just—"

"No." Oliver grabbed her hand again. "Don't go. You said you weren't invited. Well, you are now. I'm inviting you." He jutted his chin out, daring her to disagree.

Luna looked past Oliver and saw Angie standing in the doorway. Her arms were crossed over her chest, her body rigid. Luna could feel her glare across the yard. She took a deep breath, smiled, and waved.

Oliver tugged her sleeve again. "Come on."

"You might as well join us. Can't possibly make things any worse." Jack patted her shoulder, and Luna liked his practical approach to the upcoming train wreck.

"Yeah, I guess." Luna squared her shoulders and followed Oliver.

❖

"You didn't eat very much." Luna sat next to Angie.

It was the first time all afternoon they'd been alone, and Angie was almost surprised when Luna spoke. She'd carefully avoided Angie until that point.

Angie shrugged. "Not hungry." She was still fuming over Luna's appearance at her family gathering.

"I didn't plan this, you know." Luna ran her knuckles over the back of Angie's hand. Despite her anger, Angie's body responded. She pulled her hand away.

Angie started to stand. She wasn't interested in Luna's explanation.

"Angie," Luna grabbed her hand, "please, wait."

"For what, Luna? We talked about this, then you show up at my home uninvited, insinuate your way into a *family* function, and you've sat there acting like you belong." Angie ticked the items off on her finger. The hurt on Luna's face made Angie pause, but it didn't stop her. "You don't get to do that, Luna. You just don't."

Luna's expression flashed from hurt to anger and back to hurt. "It's not like that. I told you, I didn't plan to come here. Your son dragged me inside." Luna pushed her hands through her hair. "I *tried* to leave, damn it."

"Not hard enough." Angie stood and placed her hands on the table. "Better yet, you shouldn't have showed up here." Angie wanted to yell and scream until Luna understood. It was bad enough to have her father grilling her for information. She didn't want Oliver getting attached this early in their relationship. It wouldn't be fair to him. She forced herself to keep her voice level. "How the hell did that happen anyway?"

"I told you. I was frustrated and went for a walk. I didn't think about where I was going. When I looked up, I was here."

"You still should have left."

Luna threw her arms up. "Why?"

"What do you mean *why*? Do you make a habit of showing up at people's houses uninvited?"

"Why wasn't I invited?" Luna's voice trembled slightly. "Perez was, for Christ's sake. Why wasn't I?"

"I didn't know Tori did that." Angie looked at her lap. The hurt in Luna's eyes made more sense now. Angie wondered how long Luna had been chewing on the inequity.

"You're avoiding the question."

"Luna, this is where I live." Angie made a sweeping gesture with her arms.

"Yes." Luna stepped close and took Angie's hands. "I want to know all of you, especially here."

Angie melted just a little, but refused to lose sight of her original objection. "You don't understand. *Oliver* lives here."

"I want to know him, too."

How could she explain to Luna that she had to protect Oliver? That she didn't want Oliver to get attached and then get his heart broken when Luna flaked on him? Luna wouldn't understand.

"That's sweet, really it is, and maybe someday we can do something about that, but right now it's still too soon." Angie took a deep breath. "If Perez and Tori never see each other after today, it won't make a difference to Oliver. What I do, what *you* do, could hurt him."

Before Luna could respond, the others joined them on the deck again.

Even though their discussion was rather loud at times, Angie chose to believe that it took place in a bubble of isolation and that Oliver couldn't possibly have overheard them through the open door. Angie dropped into her seat and tugged her hand free of Luna's grip. The subject was closed.

"Luna," Jack smiled, "I don't know anything about you. Start with your childhood and work forward from there."

"Wow. No pressure." Luna wiped her hands on her jeans.

"I'm kidding. Tell me something simple, like about your work."

Angie laughed on the inside. She had no idea how much Jack would enjoy playing the protective father. This was the first time he'd had the opportunity.

"I own a small business, but we are expanding." Luna's foot twitched nervously and Angie almost felt sorry for her. Almost. Luna got herself into this, she could get herself out.

"Yes, but what do you *do*?"

Jack knew damn good and well what Luna did. Angie had told him.

Sandy tugged the front of her bustier to the side and revealed a rose. "Tattoos. She did this one."

"Oh, yeah." Luna looked closer and nodded. "I thought you looked familiar."

Angie took Luna's hand. On top of everything else, her girlfriend had seen her father's girlfriend topless. It was her very own fucked-up version of seven degrees of separation.

Jack continued his interrogation. "Why tattoos, Luna?"

Luna laced her fingers with Angie's and pulled her hand into her lap. "I had to do something with my MFA, and starving artist just didn't sound appealing."

"MFA?" Jack asked.

"Master of Fine Arts. It was easier than the engineering degree my mom wanted me to get."

"You have a master's?" Angie shook her head, certain she'd heard Luna wrong. Luna gave people tattoos for a living. She wasn't curator at the Portland Art Museum. How the hell did she end up with an MFA? Until thirty seconds ago, Angie would have sworn there was some snooty restriction involving leather and advanced degrees. Luna had dropped her beliefs through a blender and suddenly she was inside a Picasso painting. All the expected parts were there, but she couldn't make sense of it.

"Don't look so surprised."

"Do you have a degree, Perez?" She had to find the reverse button that would undo the brain-scramble, or she'd have to create a new world order in her head, one where tattooing was a perfectly legitimate occupation and leather-wearing women weren't destined to give her moral cavities.

"Yeah, but only a BA. I ran out of money before I finished my master's. Besides, Luna agreed to take me on as an apprentice. That's worth more than a MFA in the tattoo world."

"Really?"

"Close." Perez nodded. "Luna's the best."

"I'm okay." Luna squeezed Angie's hand.

Oliver pointed to the angel on Luna's bicep and said, "Who did your tattoo, Luna?"

Angie didn't like how fixated Oliver was on Luna's tattoo. He was too young to start the argument over permanent body art.

Luna scratched lightly over the image. "I did."

"Cool." Oliver sat back like that decided everything.

"How is that possible?" Angie couldn't even draw a proper stick person on a stationary piece of paper. A tattoo on her own arm would look like a cracked-out connect-the-dots—good intentions, but crappy results.

"Mirror and tons of patience."

"What about family?" Jack asked.

Angie wondered if he was checking off a mental list of questions.

"Not much to tell. There's just me."

"Impossible," Jack said. "You didn't just appear on the planet, full-grown and ready for life."

Angie was interested in her answer. Other than a few fleeting statements about her mom, Luna hadn't shared much about family.

Luna shrugged.

"Mother, father, brothers, sisters?" Perhaps Jack thought Luna didn't know exactly what family was.

"I'm an only child." Luna sank into her chair and rested her sunglasses over her eyes.

Jack was undeterred. "Father?"

"Never met him."

Angie scooted her chair closer to Luna's and rested her hand on Luna's arm, smoothing her thumb back and forth. So far Luna was doing great. Not that Angie should care how well they all got along. She didn't plan to invite Luna back.

"Really? You don't know anything about him?"

Jack was starting to irritate Angie. Did he realize he was coming across like an asshole?

"Mom said he was a plumber from Jersey. She moved here before I was born. He stayed there."

Everyone else remained quiet throughout their exchange. Angie was amazed. Oliver and Tori should be playing video games by now, and Sandy should be making noise about leaving. The woman couldn't stand to be off her Harley for too long on sunny days. Angie had no idea what Perez would normally be doing at this point, but she wouldn't be sitting quietly while others talked. The impending disaster of Jack giving Luna the third degree was simply too much to ignore.

"And what about your mom, Luna?" Jack took a drink and regarded Luna over the top of his bottle. "Angie, have you met her?"

"She died nine years ago," Luna finally answered. "I'd been out of school for a year."

Angie did the math. If Luna finished her bachelor's at twenty-two, her master's at twenty-three—unlikely considering it took the average person longer—that made Luna a minimum of thirty-three. She was at least six years older than Angie.

"I'm sorry." Jack seemed satisfied. Perhaps he realized that he'd asked too much.

"It was a long time ago." Luna shrugged, but her body was still tense.

"Who wants dessert?" Angie stood, hoping Luna would follow her to the kitchen. She didn't move. "I'll be right back."

Inside the kitchen, she could hear that regular conversation had resumed around the table. She prepared strawberry shortcakes for everyone, trayed them up, and headed outside with a vague flash of being at work on her day off.

She served everyone and took the remaining one for herself. Luna offered her a small smile as she took a bite.

"Luna." Oliver scooted closer. "Guess where Mom and Grandpa are taking me next weekend? Oaks Park."

Jack cleared his throat. "I've been meaning to talk to you about that."

Angie braced herself. She was accustomed to Jack bailing at the last minute. Oliver, however, had been essentially blanketed from that. "What happened, Dad?"

"I got a job. It's just a couple of days, but next Saturday is one of them." Jack picked up odd jobs wherever he could. Since Oliver was born, he'd tried to arrange his schedule around Angie's, and in the past couple of years, he'd worked less and less. Passing on an opportunity, no matter how small, was just not an option. "I planned to tell you later today."

Oliver jutted out his chin and crossed his arms. "That sucks."

"Why don't you ask Luna to join you?" Jack poked his fork toward Luna.

Angie shook her head and took a deep breath. She wasn't sure how to explain her concerns in a way Oliver would understand.

Luna placed her hand on Angie's leg and stroked gently over her thigh. "That's not a good idea."

Oliver's face fell. "Why not?"

Luna shrugged and removed her hand.

"How 'bout we go, just the two of us, Oli?"

"But I like Luna. I want her to go."

"I don't think so, son." Angie spoke quietly.

Jack put a hand on Oliver's arm to stop him from speaking. Oliver glared at Angie and took a bite of his strawberry shortcake, then chewed with angry, exaggerated movements.

Angie didn't want this argument. The day, while tense at times, had been just about perfect. A door-slamming tantrum from Oliver would ruin it.

"Mom—"

"Oliver, enough." Angie used her best mom voice. Firm, but not screechy. It didn't always work, but she hoped Oliver would hold himself in check since they had company.

Oliver ran to his room and slammed the door. On his way he yelled, "It's not always about you, you know!"

Angie debated following him, but opted to let him cool off before she tried to talk to him. She smiled at everyone. "Sorry about that."

Luna returned the smile but still looked sad. "It's okay, I understand."

"Thank you." Sometimes being a mom was exhausting.

"Luna, did your mom ever marry?" Jack was back to grilling Luna. Given Oliver's outburst, there really weren't any comfortable topics, but this one certainly didn't help.

"No. I don't think she even dated."

"Really?" Jack whistled. "I can't imagine going twenty-four years without...companionship."

"I don't know for sure." Luna fidgeted with the label on her beer, peeling back one corner. "If she did, she did it without me knowing."

"Why?"

"She didn't want me to get attached or something." The label was halfway off.

"What did you want?"

"I wanted her to be happy." Luna kept her eyes focused over Jack's shoulder. "I felt guilty that I kept her from meeting someone."

"Hear that, Angie?" Jack resumed his campaign for Angie to involve Luna in their lives more.

As bad as she felt about what Luna was saying, Angie still hated the constant parade of new women through her dad's bedroom. They made noises she didn't want to hear and left the next morning with their heels in their hand. "I hear, Dad."

"You should take your son to Oaks Park. And you should take Luna with you." Jack gave up circling his point and zeroed in on it.

"Dad, I—"

"You want that boy to think you've sacrificed everything for him? That's a lot of guilt to saddle him with."

"It's better than having him think he's in the way." Angie regretted the words as soon as they were out. It was too late to change anything now, so why bring it up?

"So you trade one for the other? Oliver deserves better, Angie." Her father's voice softened. "You deserved better. I just didn't know how to give it to you."

"You did the best you could." She gave herself this answer any time she tried to reconcile the screwed-up things Jack did when she was little with his almost perfect devotion to Oliver.

"I really did, but you're better than I ever was." Jack held her gaze. "Do the right thing for your son."

Angie nodded. At this point, she had no idea what the right thing was, but she was having a harder time seeing the harm in a day-trip to an amusement park. It wasn't Oliver's fault that Jack had to cancel. She could take him alone, but even that would feel like a punishment at this point.

"Think we should tell the others they can come back out?" Jack gestured toward the house. Angie hadn't realized that everyone else had fled the scene, leaving her and Jack to hash it out alone.

"Not yet." She finished her bottle of beer. "Tell me why this matters to you so much."

"He worries, Angie." Jack looked more serious than Angie ever remembered. "He wants you to be happy, too."

Angie didn't know what to make of Jack's assertion. Oliver didn't look worried to her. Then again, he spent more time with Jack than he did with her. Perhaps the topic of his concern about her was top secret and kept between the two of them.

"Can't I just tell him that I am?"

"It's not enough. He wants to see it."

"Okay." Against her better judgment, Angie went in search of Luna and Oliver. She might as well tell them the news at the same time.

CHAPTER TEN

Wednesday, September 9

"I really like this one." Perez held out yet another manila folder full of sketches and a personal profile. "She studied at the Art Institute and has great definition." When they moved to their new location, Perez would transition from novice to mentor. She was stressing over the selection process for her first apprentice.

The file included a head shot of the artist. The photo was irrelevant to her ability as a tattoo artist, but more than half of the applications included one. "And she's hot," Luna said. "That doesn't hurt."

"Are you allowed to notice that anymore?"

Luna closed the file. "What's that supposed to mean?"

"You're chasing a single mom. She'll have you on lockdown before you know it." Perez handed the next file to Luna.

"I wish." Luna would gladly follow whatever guidelines Angie decided to set. "But it's not likely. Angie has more important things to worry about."

Perez's playful tone disappeared. "With so many applications, how do I pick one?"

"Pick two."

"Two?"

"One for you, one for me." Luna's concession was out of character. Normally she'd be agonizing over the candidates along with Perez.

"Shit." Perez looked on the verge of panic. "How did you decide? When you selected me."

"You don't remember?" How could Perez possibly forget? When

she'd arrived for the interview, Luna had tossed her file in the trash and forced her to sketch image after image in rapid-fire succession. "You were nervous as hell, but you could still create." Perez's passion had made her impossible to ignore.

"You scared the shit out of me." Perez shuddered, then reached for another file.

Luna stopped her. "Just set up the interviews. I'll sit in."

"Great." Perez pushed the stack to the corner of the counter. "Now what?"

"Now I walk to The Cadillac and meet Angie. If I'm lucky, she'll let me escort her home." Luna punched Perez's arm lightly. "And you get to stay here and close up." Sometimes being the boss rocked.

"You nervous?"

"About?"

"Saturday," Perez said.

Saturday. Oaks Park with Angie and Oliver. "Terrified." Luna flipped through the appointment book and verified that she had nothing else scheduled that night. She didn't. On her way out the door she repeated, "Absolutely terrified."

❖

"Slow night." Angie counted out her tips. The diners had been generous, but her earnings were still lighter than usual. "I can't believe I agreed to take Sunday off to go to an anniversary party for people I don't even know." Luna had no idea how much it would cost Angie to miss a day of tips. She battled a sliver of resentment about the request, especially after Luna showed up uninvited Labor Day.

"I'm sure it's important to her." Tori rested her hip against the edge of the counter. She'd finished counting out a few minutes ago and was waiting for Angie.

"I'm sure paying the mortgage and buying groceries is important to me, too."

"Angie, it's already done. Relax and enjoy it."

Angie tucked her money into her front pocket and slipped her jacket around her shoulders. "Are you going?"

"No, I have to work."

Angie punched Tori in the arm, not appreciating her sense of humor.

"Seriously, Perez didn't mention it. I assume that means we aren't going." Tori shrugged.

"You guys have been seeing each other a lot."

Tori smiled, but her goofy, happy expression told Angie that her mind was a million miles away. "I kinda like her."

"Yeah?" Angie was happy for her.

"Yeah. What about you and Luna?"

"She's nice." Angie thought Luna was more than nice, but she forced the hopeful, yet nagging, voice to quiet down. She wasn't ready to give it full volume yet.

Tori held the front door open for Angie. "She likes you."

"How can you tell?"

"Because she's standing right there." Tori pointed to Luna, who was leaning against the wall next to the entrance.

"Hi." She held out a single rose. "I thought maybe I could walk you home. If you're talking to me, that is."

God, she had the sexiest smile. Angie took the rose and gave Luna a quick kiss. She just couldn't resist those lips. "Walking is good. Talking is negotiable."

"I can accept that." Luna tucked Angie's arm into the crook of her elbow. "Since Angie's not talking, how are you tonight, Tori?"

"On my way to see Perez. I'm doing just fine, so I can talk to you all the way to the shop." Tori's tone added innuendo to a statement that was otherwise benign, which always amazed Angie. "How about you, Luna?"

Angie eased her hand into Luna's and interlocked their fingers. She liked the romanticism of being escorted, but craved the texture and intimacy of Luna's palm against hers.

"Angie's holding my hand, so I guess I'm doing rather well." Luna squeezed it gently.

The crisp night air chilled Angie and she shivered in her lightweight jacket. Luna pulled her closer, wrapping her arm around her waist. "Cold?" She spoke quietly, her mouth turned toward Angie's ear.

"I'll be okay."

Luna didn't loosen her grip. "Better safe than sorry."

"Why are you here?"

Luna should be at Coraggio getting ready to close the shop, not surprising her after work.

"I missed you, and I wanted to see you," Luna said, then kissed Angie's hand.

They strolled in silence, holding hands and smiling. When they stopped in front of Coraggio, Tori waved at Perez through the glass.

"This has been really awkward." Tori stepped through the door Perez held open for her. "But you guys are freakin' adorable. You make me want to puke." The door swished shut behind her.

"So." Luna faced Angie. "Want to come in? Or should we continue to your house?" She looked hopeful.

What would happen if Luna walked her home? She would kiss her good night at the gate and that would be that. If they stayed here, much more would happen. Sweaty, wonderful things.

But Oliver had school tomorrow morning and he didn't deserve to have zombie-mom fix his breakfast.

"I need to get home, but I'm fine. You can stay here."

Luna gave her a gentle, nibbling kiss that made Angie rethink her plan about not following Luna up the stairs.

"I want to go with you." Luna stepped back, squeezed Angie's hand again, then started toward Angie's house.

Angie enjoyed the companionable quiet. It was enough to simply hold Luna's hand and be near her. She appreciated that Luna didn't try to fill the silence with forced banter.

The front porch light lit the path from the sidewalk to the door. Angie tried to tell Luna good-bye at the gate, but couldn't force the words. She tried again when they reached the porch, but couldn't bring herself to drop Luna's hand. It simply felt too good meshed with hers.

"Coffee?" The invitation surprised Angie. This time of night she had to be careful. Caffeine wound her up rather than helped her unwind. Still, she wanted Luna to say yes.

"You sure that's okay?" Luna ran her fingers up Angie's arms and settled her hands at the base of Angie's neck, toying with the hair that had fallen out of the sloppy bun on the back of her head. "I should go and let you get some sleep."

Luna loosened the clips and finger-combed Angie's hair as it fell around her shoulders. It felt divine. Angie groaned and let her head fall against Luna's shoulder. When she spoke, her voice was muffled. "Come inside."

This was a bad idea, but Angie didn't want Luna to stop her massage, which had moved to her neck and shoulders. She was kneading tight circles into the tension-filled muscles at the base of Angie's neck.

"God, you're tight," Luna whispered in Angie's ear. Angie wasn't sure what Luna was referring to.

Luna watched Angie fumble to unlock the door. The screen door squeaked, the deadbolt stuck, and Angie's ears flared pink. She was adorable. Luna molded her front to Angie's back, and the pleasure of being so close made her unable to resist touching her lips to the top of Angie's ear.

"Let me." Luna placed her hand over Angie's and helped her turn the key. Luna actually wanted to push Angie against the door and tear off her clothes. The thought of Angie trembling in the muted porch light, moaning Luna's name, threatened to destroy Luna's resolve. Angie might like it in the moment, but as soon as the afterglow faded, she'd be spitting mad. Luna wanted to be invited back to Angie's home, so she held herself in check.

Angie drew in a shuddering breath. It was good to know that she was affected, too. Now if she could just get Angie to admit it.

After Luna opened the door and waited for Angie to enter, Angie pushed her body back into Luna's and Luna wrapped her arms around Angie's stomach. They stood breathing each other in for several moments until finally Angie broke away.

"We should go inside."

Angie's house was warm and inviting. The living room was small, as was the kitchen, but Luna sat comfortably at the table while Angie made a pot of coffee. Life was good inside these four walls—Luna could feel it. She wished she'd had more time to explore Angie's home on Labor Day, but that event had been filled with tension. Luna had been afraid to move too far from her safe spot on the back deck.

Angie sat opposite as they waited for the coffeemaker to do its job. Luna wanted to scoot her chair closer, but the invisible wall Angie had thrown up around herself when they entered the front door stopped her.

"So how long do I have to wait?" Luna asked.

Angie gave her a lazy, sexy smile. "Wait for what?"

"To get to know you." The tiny voice in the back of Luna's head yelled, "Stop!" This conversation would only drive Angie away, and in turn she'd rush Luna out the front door.

Angie's brows pulled together. "Isn't that what we've been doing?"

"Sort of. But you have a Do Not Enter sign on large parts of your life. I want to know all of you, not just parts."

"I thought we talked about this." Angie glanced at the coffeemaker, which was still brewing.

"We did. But we didn't get to finish." Luna silently urged Angie to crack open the door and let her in.

"There's not much else to say, Luna." Angie stood from the table and crossed to the sink. She pulled two cups out of the cabinet and, without waiting for the coffeemaker to finish, she poured the coffee. The maker continued to dispense and the black liquid ran over the counter. "I like you. Isn't that enough?" She set a cup in front of Luna, then cleaned the mess from the counter with a towel.

"I like you, too. And I want it to be enough, but I don't want to feel like I'm encroaching if I see Jack or Oliver."

"You can see Jack any time you want."

Luna waited for Angie to return to the table, then moved to the chair next to hers. She took Angie's hand. "And Oliver?"

"We're taking him to Oaks Park Saturday, aren't we?" Angie's voice was almost as rigid as her posture.

And they were. Luna knew how hard it was for Angie to share that experience with her, but she didn't understand why. "And after that?"

"Luna." Angie sighed. "I don't know, but I'm trying."

"How about I take you both to dinner next week?"

"Can we talk about something else?"

Luna didn't answer. No matter what she said, it wouldn't be right. She didn't want to change the subject, so saying yes would have been a lie, but saying no would likely cause Angie to shut down even further.

Angie broke the silence. "When I was younger, my dad brought home *so many* women. I hated it. And when I found out I was pregnant with Oliver, I promised myself I wouldn't do that to him."

"I'm not a parade, Angie. I'm just one woman."

"They were all just one woman."

Did Angie want her to promise forever? Would that persuade her to open her life? Luna couldn't make that declaration. No matter how hard she was falling for Angie, she knew better than to promise permanence based on a few weeks.

"What do you think I plan to do, Angie? Leave the second he gets to know me?"

"Why is this so important to you?" Angie traced her fingers over Luna's arm. "Can't we just enjoy one another?"

Why not indeed? Luna could easily fall into Angie and never surface. Even at the end of the day, with the beginning of dark circles below her eyes, her hair askew, and her clothes rumpled from a shift at work, Angie was beautiful. From the flirtatious half-smile that said she *might*, to the little dent in her bottom lip that Luna wanted to suck for hours, to the fluttering pulse at the base of her neck, just above the collar of her shirt—all were things in an ever-increasing catalog of Angie that made Luna smile. She could definitely enjoy Angie for a long time to come, and that's what made her want more. She caught Angie's hand and held it, rubbing her thumb easily along the half-moon between Angie's thumb and forefinger.

"Angie, I want to be someone you can count on, not just someone you show up to fuck a couple of times a week." Luna barely forced the words out. She felt too vulnerable to say what she needed at full volume.

Angie cupped her cheek, her fingers teasing along her jawline. "What if that's all I can offer right now?"

Right now. Luna clung to the words. They promised hope for more in the future.

"I guess it'll have to be enough." Luna pulled Angie to her and kissed both her eyes, the tip of her nose, and finally her lips. She lingered there, enjoying the taste of Angie, the texture of her tongue as it slipped past her teeth. The thought that this might be all they'd ever share washed Luna in sadness. She pulled away. "I should go."

Angie nodded, but rather than letting go, she kissed Luna again, her movements more urgent, more demanding. It had to be enough and that broke Luna's heart.

Luna stood, then escaped through the door, with Angie reaching for her, her mouth still shaped in a kiss.

Her coffee sat untouched on the kitchen table.

CHAPTER ELEVEN

Thursday, September 10

Angie didn't believe in God, but if heaven was real, it involved Luna's hands and a bottle of hot oil. "God, that feels so good."

Luna worked the knots in Angie's back, working the sore muscles until she felt like a pile of goo.

"Why are you so tense?" Luna's voice washed over Angie, low and seductive. Angie let her stress float away.

"Oliver's been a pain this week." *A pain* didn't begin to cover it. School had been in session for a week and Oliver had already been sent to the principal's office twice. Once because Oliver refused to come in from recess, and the second time because he was disruptive during class. Military school was looking appealing.

Luna stopped rubbing her shoulders. "What'd he do?"

Luna's sincere interest in Oliver confused Angie. Girlfriends weren't genuinely concerned about their lover's children. At least that's how Angie's childhood had played out. No matter how many times Luna asked after Oliver, Angie was still surprised.

"Trouble at school. I don't want to talk about it." Angie shimmied her shoulders, prompting Luna to resume the massage. "Less talk, more touch."

Luna hesitated, then rubbed small, soft circles on her spine.

"I love the way you make me feel."

"Yeah?" Luna's voice cracked, betraying how much Angie's answer mattered.

"Yeah." No one had ever pampered Angie the way Luna did. She felt cherished.

"You look beautiful." Luna spoke into Angie's ear, her voice even lower than usual. "Can I keep you like this?"

"Naked and oiled up?" Angie joked. "Okay, but you'll have to explain it to my boss."

"He won't mind, and your tips will skyrocket."

Angie laughed but didn't respond. It was sweet of Luna to say she was beautiful, and when she was with Luna, Angie believed it. But in the real world Angie had stretch marks on her tummy, boobs that sat an inch or two south of where they belonged, and her ass was on the verge of requiring a warning sticker because of its width. Gravity hadn't fully betrayed her yet, but she was well on her way. On top of that, her tan was fading. Shopping for school clothes with Oliver tapped into the special part of her budget reserved for pampering activities like tanning.

"Do you ever think about your dad?" She shouldn't ask, but she needed to switch the focus. Sex would have worked just as well, but she wasn't ready for the massage to be over.

"Not really." Luna smoothed her palms over Angie's low back, stretching the tight muscles. "You?"

"I think about my dad all the time. Kinda hard not to when he's planted in my kitchen most of the day."

"I meant your mom."

"Sometimes, but it makes me grumpy, so I try not to."

"Your dad's a pretty good cook."

Angie made a mental note to kiss Luna in thanks later for changing the subject. "He's great, but the cooking gene totally passed me by."

"You realize it's not genetic, it's practice." Luna worked her way over Angie's thighs. Sex was looking better with every oil-drenched inch.

"I'd rather blame my DNA. Then I'll have an excuse not to try." Angie answered with more of a moan than actual words.

"But Oliver likes to cook?"

"Oliver likes to do anything his grandpa does." Angie shuddered.

"You say that like it's a bad thing."

"My dad has some bad habits."

"Like what?" Luna reached Angie's feet and rubbed circles into the arch with her thumbs.

Angie groaned. "I'd rather Oliver not make finding the perfect marijuana a high priority. And I wouldn't complain if he dated the same woman for longer than three months." Angie closed her eyes and focused on the amazing things Luna was doing to her feet. "And if he ever shows up at his kid's school in drag—"

"He did that?" Luna sounded shocked. Maybe disbelieving.

It took Angie a moment to realize what Luna was asking about. She'd already seen Jack high. They'd talked about Jack's revolving bedroom door. That left the dresses. "Did he what? Wear a dress to my school?"

"Yeah," Luna said softly. She massaged each individual toe, rolling them gently between her thumb and fingers.

"More than once."

"I bet that fucked with your cheerleader image." Luna laughed, but she didn't sound like she meant it.

"Luna." Angie rolled onto her back. She wanted to see Luna's face. "I wasn't a cheerleader. I wasn't anything." Angie had hated high school, and she hated that the conversation had taken this turn.

"I find that hard to believe."

"My ten-year reunion is coming up. You can see for yourself then." The half-witted invitation was out before Angie could stop herself. Fuck it. If Luna was determined to turn a good time into a relationship, she could handle Angie assuming her time for boring, obligatory functions.

"You'd take me with you?" Luna resumed her massage on the front of Angie's legs.

"I sure as hell ain't going alone."

Luna laughed and tickled her way up Angie's sides. "So this is just your evil plan to torture me?"

"You're on to me."

Angie's cell phone rang, interrupting Luna's tickle onslaught.

"I have to get that." Angie ran into the kitchen and fished her phone out of her purse. It was Oliver's school. "Hello?" She fought to keep her breathing even so she wouldn't sound like a giggling teenager.

"Angie Dressen?" The man paused for Angie to acknowledge her identity. "This is Randy Payton, the assistant principal at Endeavor Elementary. I'm calling about Oliver."

Angie hated the name of Oliver's school. It sounded like he was getting his education on a starship, though she didn't think Randy Payton would appreciate her insights. "How can I help you, Mr. Payton?"

"I have Oliver here in my office and was hoping you could come talk with the two of us."

She could hear Oliver in the background yelling about being framed. "I'll be there as quickly as I can." She disconnected the call. Framed or not, Oliver was so grounded for ending her massage.

Luna stood just inside the bedroom slowly removing her clothing. The shower was running in the bathroom. "You need to wash off all that oil before you go anywhere. I'll join you."

Angie thought about arguing, but figured it was fair for Luna to assume shower time since Angie assumed Luna's attendance at her high-school reunion. "We need to hurry."

Luna ushered Angie into the shower. "And I'm driving you. Don't argue. It'll be faster."

Angie bristled. Showering together was one thing, but a trip to Oliver's school to see the assistant principal was quite another. As much as she didn't like Luna forcing herself into yet another private family moment, the practical offer of a ride won out. She needed to get to Oliver sooner rather than later. She'd decide how she felt about Luna after she finished throttling her son.

Oliver slouched in a high-backed wooden chair outside the assistant principal's office. If she ignored the scowl on his face, Angie could see the sweet little boy he used to be. But during the past year, his desire for independence and his discontent had overshadowed the sweetness. Angie didn't remember feeling the constant craving for more, the unsure anticipation about what came next, until she was at least thirteen. She felt robbed of three good years without continuous friction, but who should she file her complaint with? Probably herself, since she was the one responsible for Oliver.

Oliver was glaring unwavering at the floor, his clothes rumpled and one shoe missing.

"Hey." Angie nudged his foot and he looked up.

"Hi, Mom." He didn't sound contrite, but at least he didn't sound combative. Angie decided to count it as a victory. Oliver looked past Angie and his eyes lit up when he saw Luna standing behind her. "Luna!"

The door to Mr. Payton's office opened and the man himself poked his head out. "Ms. Dressen, thank you for coming so quickly. Please come in."

He stepped out of the way while Angie entered, then he looked expectantly at Luna. "Are you joining us?"

Angie tilted her head to the side and waited. She wanted to hear Luna's answer.

"I think I'll keep Oliver company." She sat in the chair next to his.

What Luna really should have done was wait in the car, but when she'd climbed out of the driver's side, then held the passenger door open for Angie, she'd automatically latched on to Luna. Angie found comfort in the light impression of Luna's palm against her low back. It calmed her.

"Okay." So much for limiting the amount of time Luna spent with Oliver.

The door closed, leaving Luna alone with a silent and sulking Oliver. She couldn't believe Angie hadn't stopped her from entering the building with her, or that she left the decision about joining them in the office totally up to her. It had to have been a test. Had she passed?

After several moments, Oliver finally spoke. "Mom's pissed, isn't she?"

"I don't know if that's the right term. I think she's worried more than anything else."

Oliver sat up slightly. "She looks pissed."

"Maybe she is." Luna was not an expert on Angie's emotions.

"Aren't you going to ask me what I did?"

"Do you want to tell me?"

Oliver snorted. "Not really, but Mom will even if I don't."

"Don't count on it." Luna didn't mean to say it. Oliver didn't need to know how frustrating his mother was.

"I drew on my arm." Oliver squirmed side to side in his chair.

That was it? Granted, Luna wasn't a parent, but this seemed an extreme reaction on the school's part for some non-permanent body art. Maybe it was not just that he did it. "What did you draw?"

"An angel." Oliver pushed his sleeve up. He had a decent rendition of the angel on Luna's upper arm, only his was on his left arm and Luna's was on her right.

"That's good." She traced her fingers over the ink. Oliver's work was solid, the lines clean.

"Yeah? I gave one to my buddy Josh, too." Oliver smiled. He looked like a completely different person when he wore a happy expression.

"So why did your mom get called? I'm just not seeing it." Maybe the school thought the angel was a gang sign or something.

Oliver's scowl returned. "We kinda tried to give one to another kid," he mumbled.

"And?"

"He didn't want it."

Assault by ballpoint pen. The implications offended Luna. Tattoos were highly personal. Forcing another person to wear one against his will was inconceivable. She was sure there were worse things, but she couldn't think of any. "Why?"

Oliver shrugged. "I don't know."

"You *need* to know."

Oliver chewed his bottom lip. "It started out as a joke. We were just messing around."

"How'd it go from messing around to sitting outside the vice principal's office waiting for your mom to show up?"

"He said he didn't want it, and that would have been okay. But then he said it was stupid, that the angel was dumb and anyone who had one was dumb. It made me mad."

The taunt hurt Luna to hear, which surprised her. Why would the insecure teasing of a ten-year-old boy bother a thirty-three-year-old woman? Probably because the angel was more than just a tattoo for Luna. It was her mother.

"That's no excuse." Luna was still horrified that Oliver had tried to forcibly apply the angel to the other boy's arm. "Tattoos are special. Abusing the art form like that…it's a terrible thing to do."

Oliver looked miserable. "I'm sorry."

"You can't ever, *ever*, do anything like that again." This conversation was Angie's to have with Oliver, but Luna couldn't stop herself from admonishing him. "I cannot tolerate it."

"I won't." Oliver shifted closer to Luna. "I promise." The words came out as a choked whisper and Oliver started crying.

Luna hesitated. What the hell was she supposed to do with a crying ten-year-old? Finally, she pulled him into a hug, and he threw his arms around her and buried his face in her neck.

Angie exited the office and Oliver sat up, his eyes and nose red and running.

"I'll take him home now. Thank you again for the phone call." Angie shook the man's hand. "It was nice meeting you. I hope next time it'll be under better circumstances."

The man smiled like he'd won a prize and Luna crackled with jealousy. She wanted to bark at the man until he stepped away from *her* girlfriend.

"Come on, Oliver." Angie waited for him to stand, then followed him through the corridor.

When they were locked safely inside the car, Angie exploded. "What the hell were you *thinking,* Oliver?" She didn't wait for him to answer. "They took that other boy to the hospital. The *hospital!*" She pushed her hand through her hair and blew out a sigh.

Luna took advantage of the slight lull and asked, "Your house?"

Angie nodded.

"I'm sorry, Mom." Oliver huddled in the backseat, gulping back hiccups and tears.

"Sorry isn't good enough, son. You're lucky the other parents didn't want to press charges."

Luna glanced in the rearview mirror. Oliver's face paled at his mother's observation. "Charges?" His chin trembled.

Luna drove as fast as possible. She didn't want to speed with Oliver and Angie in the car, but she didn't want to prolong this experience.

"What am I going to do with you?" Angie's voice was tired. Luna wanted to comfort her, hold her while she fell asleep.

"It won't happen again."

"Damn right it won't. You've been suspended for a week while they decide what to do. Do you realize they could kick you out?"

Luna pulled into Angie's driveway and killed the engine. She'd made it there in record time. As Oliver exited the car, Luna grasped Angie's hand, holding her back.

"Can I come in with you?" She'd already pushed her luck at the school This time she asked before following Angie inside.

"It's probably a bad idea."

Angie wasn't rushing to send her away. Luna's internal cheerleader did a flip in spite of the horrible circumstances.

"Probably, but I want to anyway." It was Angie's night off and Luna wanted to be there to hold her when she cried.

"Did he tell you what he did?"

"He showed me his arm." Luna brushed the backs of her fingers against Angie's cheek, then worked her hand down to cup the side of Angie's neck.

"It looks like yours, doesn't it?" Angie ran her hand beneath Luna's sleeve and palmed the angel.

"Close." Luna didn't like where this conversation was going.

"Did he tell you why he did it?"

"He said the other boy made fun of him, told him his angel was stupid."

Angie pushed the sleeve up and kissed Luna's tattoo. "It's not stupid."

"No, but forcing someone into a tattoo he doesn't want? That's not okay." *Not okay* was the understatement of the year for Luna. She was trying not to freak out.

"Thank God it's not permanent."

"How bad was he hurt?"

"Not at all." Angie offered a tired smile.

Luna was confused. "You said hospital."

"I may have exaggerated for dramatic effect. I want Oliver to think about what he's done."

"I believe he is sorry." Luna wondered how much further this conversation would go before Angie remembered she was talking to Luna, the woman she didn't want influencing her son. Especially since it was her angel that Oliver had copied. She was afraid if she left now, Angie might never let her back in.

"Yeah, but is that enough?"

"I don't know." Luna shook her head. She loved Angie's strength, her commitment to her son. Even more, she loved that Angie was letting her share this moment of difficulty, letting Luna see her struggle. For the first time, Luna wanted to be strong for someone else.

"I should get inside." Angie reached for the door handle.

Back to Luna's original question. "Can I come with you?"

"Not this time." Angie gave Luna a brief kiss. "As much as I'd rather be with you, I need to deal with this."

"I wouldn't interfere."

"I know, but I don't want to drag you into my family drama any deeper than you already are." Angie exited the car and crossed the yard.

Luna watched until she disappeared into the house, then started the car and backed out of the driveway. What could she do to make her intentions clearer for Angie?

CHAPTER TWELVE

Friday, September 11

Angie paced the linoleum floor in the kitchen. She was tired of arguing with her father. "Nothing you can say will make this okay, Dad. Nothing."

"He's ten years old, Angie. Boys make mistakes." Jack sipped his coffee. He was acting like Oliver had done nothing more serious than graffiti a bathroom stall.

"This wasn't a *mistake*. It was *assault*." Angie thrust her words out like mental battering rams, hoping they would somehow break through Jack's stubborn refusal to face reality. "What am I supposed to say to the other boy's parents?" Angie didn't want to have that conversation, but she couldn't avoid it. If their roles were reversed, she'd want answers. They deserved the same.

"I don't know, Angie." Jack pulled a box out of the cupboard above the refrigerator. It was behind an assortment of vases and he had to use a stool to get it. Then he sat at the table and emptied the contents onto the table. It was an elaborate kit for rolling joints. Angie had never seen it before. Jack's fingers trembled slightly as he worked the paper. Maybe he was more upset than he was letting on.

"Do you have to do that *now*?" Angie needed to focus on her son, not her aging father's lingering Peter Pan complex.

"Yes, I do." Jack sparked the joint and sucked in a mouthful of smoke. After a long pause, he exhaled and offered it to Angie. "You probably should, too."

"Christ, Dad." Angie flipped on the exhaust fan over the stove, cracked the window above the sink, and opened the back door. She stood just outside the door and continued with her previous line of thought. "Maybe I should put him in counseling."

"Do you really think that's necessary?"

Angie didn't want to, but she couldn't ignore the seriousness of Oliver's actions. "It probably doesn't matter what I think. The school may require it in order for him to go back."

"I didn't think about that." Jack took another hit, and his body relaxed slightly.

"You realize it matches Luna's tattoo?" Angie hated the correlation. She was getting used to having Luna in her life, but if it was hurting Oliver, she would give her up.

"I figured."

"What should I do about that?" She didn't know why she was asking Jack's opinion. He made decisions with his libido, or through marijuana-tinted glasses.

"Why would you do anything?"

"Would Oliver have done this without her influence?" Angie knew her question was absurd before she'd said it. Luna had spent hardly any time with Oliver, and if he was about to have a violent outburst at school, it would have happened with or without Luna and her angel.

"This exactly? Probably not." Jack was staring hard at the burning tip of his joint. "But he might have done something else. Angie, don't use this as an excuse to deny yourself companionship. You don't deserve to be punished. It isn't your fault."

"Then whose fault is it?" Of course it was her fault.

"Oliver is growing up. He's trying to figure out what to do with all that extra energy and confusion rolling around inside him." Jack shrugged, apparently back to trying to convince Angie it was no big deal.

"I need to spend more time with him. Maybe I could switch to mornings?"

"Can you afford that?" They'd had this conversation too many times in the past. Jack knew tips were better at dinnertime.

"Probably not." Angie slumped against the door frame, feeling helpless. "Maybe I should pull him out of baseball."

"What would that solve?"

"I don't know." Angie loved that Oliver played baseball, possibly more than Oliver. Still, he was excited when his coach proposed a special program that continued play long after the regular season ended. "But he needs to know that his behavior has consequences."

"And having his mom called to the principal's office isn't a consequence?" Jack held out his joint to Angie. She'd never accepted his offer and didn't know why he kept trying. Perhaps he thought she was really missing out, or maybe it was force of habit from years of getting stoned with friends.

"Is it enough?" Angie rubbed her temples and wished she were with Luna and her magic bottle of massage oil. That would be far better than trying to determine the right way to curb Oliver's aggressive tendencies.

"Have you talked to him, Angie?"

"No, but Luna did."

"Really? Where were you?"

"Inside the assistant principal's office. It was worse than being called there as a student."

"I bet." Jack chuckled. "Did he say why he did it?"

"The boy called his angel *stupid*." Angie couldn't quite follow Oliver's progression. How did a disagreement over a fake tattoo escalate to Oliver's friend Josh pinning a smaller boy while Oliver drew on his arm? Mr. Payton said no one was seriously injured, but the boy's shirt was ripped. Angie would have to replace that.

"So he was defending something he knew was precious to Luna," Jack surmised.

"But that doesn't make sense. He's only seen it a couple of times, and beyond saying that she did it herself and that it hurt, she's never said anything about it being important to her."

"She touches it anytime someone mentions her mother."

"You think Oliver made that connection?"

"Maybe, maybe not. But the way she guards it, covering it with her hand? That would have registered. Perhaps not consciously, but enough to make him want to protect it the way she does."

Her chest tightened. "Now I'm back to not seeing Luna again."

"Don't be silly, Angie. She's a good woman, despite your efforts to paint her otherwise. Let her help you instead of pushing her away."

"I don't want her to hurt Oliver."

"She won't."

"She might."

Jack took another hit. "What are you afraid of?"

Angie debated telling Jack the truth. Did she really want to reveal her concerns to him? "She reminds me too much of your girlfriends. I don't want to be with someone like that."

"She reminds you…" After Jack's voice tapered off, it came back stronger than ever. "Angie, you're an idiot if you think she's anything like the women I date."

"She's completely wild and untamed." The thought made Angie's breath catch in her throat. She pictured Luna naked and lying above her, hair cascading over her in loose tangles, a sheen of sweat covering her body, her eyes inviting and dangerous. She banished the image and continued ticking off the similarities Luna shared with her father's line of women. "She does tattoos for a living, looks like a porn star, and owns more cow hide than a dairy farm. That's not All-American wholesome. Not to mention, the longest relationship she's ever been in was based solely on sex, and she has a reputation for being promiscuous."

"That's ridiculous. What's the longest relationship you've been in, Angie? The last few months with Luna is the only one I can think of past high school, so you're just as bad with demonstrated commitment. And you want to talk about promiscuous? You had Oliver when you were seventeen. Immaculate conception, while a popular subject amongst the Christians, is impossible. She owns her own business, which she is expanding. By all accounts, that makes her successful." Jack stubbed out his joint and tossed it into the garbage disposal, then crossed the room and grasped Angie by the shoulders. "All that leaves is the leather pants. Are you really going to throw away the chance to be happy with a woman who adores you based on clothing?"

Angie sighed. When put that way, her fears seemed damn silly. Silly or not, she still wasn't ready to fully embrace her growing feelings for Luna, let alone examine the possibility of love.

❖

Saturday, September 12

"You know you have appointments this afternoon?" Perez tapped the appointment book.

"I'll be back in time." Luna couldn't believe Angie was allowing Oliver the trip to Oaks Park, given his recent altercation at school. She was doubly surprised that she was still invited. Absolutely no way would she cancel now. She might have to cut the day shorter than she'd like to make it to work on time, but that was no reason to skip it altogether. Angie would understand. Hopefully Oliver would as well.

"The first one is at four."

"I know." One more reminder and Luna might roll up the appointment book and smack Perez on the nose with it.

"Okay. I just don't want to be the one sitting here when Clarissa walks in and you're still out on your play date."

Clarissa Waters, one of Luna's regular clients, had an endless desire for ink and a similarly endless supply of funds to fuel her obsession. She was also a royal pain in the ass. Her temper was perpetually at 99.9 degrees Celsius and the tiniest thing made her boil over. Once Luna offered her a register receipt, rather than a handwritten one with the description of the work done, and Clarissa threw a massive temper tantrum. She didn't calm until Ruby stormed down the stairs and out-hissy-fitted her. Trust-fund babies spoke a language all their own, one that Luna would never understand.

"Perez, do not make me say it again. I'll be here." Luna ground her teeth.

"Okay." Perez closed the appointment book.

"Okay."

"Are you picking them up?" Perez asked.

Luna looked at the clock. "Yep, in about twenty minutes."

"You excited?"

"Nervous. I can't believe she agreed to let me come." Luna shook her head slightly. Apparently, Jack had some sort of magic ability to change Angie's mind. Luna needed to learn his secrets.

"What about tomorrow?" Perez dragged the stack of files from the bottom desk drawer.

Luna cringed. She didn't want to look at applications for

apprentices. "She said yes. You bringing Tori?" If Perez had invited Tori to Nan and Vi's anniversary party it wouldn't be so boring for Angie.

"Yep." Perez flipped open the top file. "She's pissed that I waited until the last minute, but she's coming."

"Good." Luna scrambled to distract Perez from the applications. "Did you make the appointment with the realtor?"

"I tried. Called the realtor about fifty times. Kept getting kicked to voice mail."

"Fifty? You're kidding." Luna knew Perez was obsessive, but that many calls in a day landed her squarely in stalkerville. "You'll end up with a restraining order, not an appointment."

"No, I won't." Perez stared hard at Luna. "We've looked at this place, it's perfect. I don't want to miss out because our realtor is spending the day at the beach. Literally or metaphorically."

"That makes no sense." Luna let Perez's exaggeration pass. Yes, they'd looked at the exterior of the building, even peered through the windows to check out the basic layout. So far, it did appear perfect, but they hadn't actually *looked* at it, not with any amount of critical objectivity. Perez had been so excited to find a place that met all their criteria, at least on paper, and Luna was in serious denial about moving. Neither of them was able to evaluate the actual pros and cons of the location. "One message is enough to get your point across. Now she'll think we're crazy."

"Luna, you're not allowed to talk yourself out of this."

Luna didn't answer. The idea of moving Coraggio still gave her twinges of guilt. Intellectually she knew it was the right thing, but emotionally, she was clinging to their current location.

"You find an apprentice?" Luna asked. Discussing would-be tattoo artists would be her penance for frustrating Perez over the real estate.

"I've narrowed it to four." She laid out the sample sheets of art work. "And I need to know when you want to talk to them."

Luna checked the clock again. Ten minutes until Angie expected her. "Just schedule them in the book. Any time, I don't care." She grabbed her jacket. "I gotta run. Wish me luck." She waved to Perez on her way out the door.

When Luna pulled up in front of Angie's house, she froze, unsure what to do next. Should she wait in the car? Should she go to the door? Should she have bought flowers? She was nervous as hell. Angie would never forgive her if she fucked this up. For that matter, Luna would never forgive herself.

Finally, she took a deep breath and opened the door. As she was climbing out of the car, her elbow bumped the steering wheel. The horn sounded louder than she ever remembered, and she jumped, victim of jangled nerves and embarrassment. She sprinted to the door. God forbid Angie thought she was the kind of asshole that honked the horn and waited in the driveway.

Oliver burst through the front door and stopped, close enough that Luna braced for impact. She thought Oliver intended to jump on her and was surprised when he held back. He vibrated with excitement.

"Hi, Luna," Oliver said with an enormous smile.

"Hey." Luna indulged the urge to ruffle his hair. Surprisingly, he didn't resist. "Your mom inside?"

"Yeah, along with my friend Josh. Mom said he could go, too. If it's okay with you." Oliver bounced in place. "Is it? Is it okay?"

Oliver's energy level was giving Luna a slight headache. Having his friend along would either double the intensity of her pain or provide Oliver with another outlet for his enthusiasm. She was about to find out. "That's okay by me."

"Yes." Oliver jumped into the air and pumped his fist.

Luna looked over to see Angie standing on the front porch. Wearing a loose white button-down shirt, faded jeans with a hole in one knee, and the sweetest smile Luna had ever seen, Angie took her breath away.

Everything would be okay.

"Are you sure this is okay?" Angie held Luna's hand, letting their arms swing in unison between them as they walked toward the entrance of Oaks Park. The family-centric amusement park probably wasn't the best venue for lesbian displays of affection, but Angie liked the way

Luna's palm felt against hers. If she intended to have a full relationship with Luna, it was time to stop holding back. She gripped Luna's hand a little tighter.

"What? This?" Luna raised their joined hands to her mouth and kissed the back of Angie's. "I'm positive."

"No, not this." Angie jostled her hand slightly. "But that's good to know, too. I was talking about them." Oliver and Josh ran ahead of them, playing tag between the parked cars. "I should have warned you that Josh was coming."

Luna shrugged. "Maybe. I'm just glad I'm here. You could have invited the entire varsity football team and the marching band, and it wouldn't matter to me."

"I almost canceled completely." Angie let the sentence hang, glad she didn't need to rehash her reasons. After all, Luna had been there.

"Why didn't you?"

"I wanted to see Josh." Angie collected her thoughts. She hadn't been able to explain why she not only wanted to continue with the outing, but to include Oliver's friend as well. "I…wanted to see them together. See if they act different."

"Than what?" Luna faced Angie and gripped her hand a little tighter. She was concerned, which made Angie smile inside.

"Than before this week." Angie couldn't force herself to describe the situation more clearly. What should she say? Before my son assaulted someone. Before the angel incident. Before… The list of possibilities was long, and every one of them made her stomach ache.

"And?" Luna probed gently.

"No difference that I can see." That bothered Angie. She wanted some clear indicator in Oliver or Josh's behavior, preferably in the form of a neon sign declaring what went wrong to cause them to cross that line. But she didn't see anything but the same two boys, sometimes sweet, sometimes surly, but with no hint of violence.

"Maybe it's there and it's just too small to notice," Luna suggested.

"Maybe." Angie released Luna's hand and dug her wallet out of her pocket. They were almost to the ticket booth. "I made him wash the tattoo off."

The boys reached the entrance and turned to wait. Oliver tapped his foot, pointed at a make-believe watch on his wrist, and scowled at Angie. Josh poked him in the side and they both burst into giggles. Angie shook her head. She still couldn't reconcile the teasing boys in front of her with their actions earlier in the week.

"That's good." Luna's simple acceptance eased Angie's mind. She'd worried that Luna would be upset, possibly think Angie's decision somehow reflected on Luna's tattoo. That wasn't the case, but it helped that Luna didn't ask her to explain or justify her reasons.

They joined the boys at the entrance and Angie paid for their ride bracelets. Luna protested, but Angie shoved her money through the slot in the window first and won the argument by default.

"Which ride do you guys want to do first?" Luna fiddled with the red plastic band around her wrist.

"The scream-n-eagle!" both boys yelled at once.

Angie stared at the ride in question, which looked like a surefire ticket to vomitsville. She pointed to a more sedate ride. "How about the carousel?"

"Oh, Mom." Oliver kicked the ground.

"Come on, Angie, we want to go on the cool rides." Luna nudged her arm. Angie could tell Oliver's excitement was beginning to rub off on her.

"You want to go on the scream-n-eagle?" Angie couldn't believe it. Not a single adult was on it. They were waiting in a circle around the ride.

"Yeah, Perez and I came here last year. It was a blast."

Angie shrugged her defeat and motioned for them to go. "I'll wait here."

She watched as Luna joked and laughed along with Oliver and Josh as they stood in line. She stole Oliver's ball cap and put in on her own head. Oliver leaped up and stole it back. Luna laughed, pointed to their right in an exaggerated look-over-there gesture, then swiped Josh's when they looked away. Josh didn't protest her wearing it, but gave her a sloppy, puppy-dog look. He smiled and told her she could keep it.

"Nah, I'm okay." Luna dropped the hat back on his head, then looked over at Angie and winked.

Angie wished for her camera as the three climbed on board the ride. She wanted to capture Luna mid-hurl. Gross for an I-told-you-so moment, but since Oliver was born, Angie's threshold for disgusting was amazingly high.

Surprisingly, Luna didn't puke, but Oliver did. Six steps away from the ride, Oliver's face paled, he clamped his hand over his mouth, and ran for the nearest trash can. Luna chased him.

"You okay, buddy?" Luna rubbed big circles on Oliver's back.

Oliver nodded and wiped his mouth with the back of his sleeve. Angie cringed.

Josh teased Oliver. "That's gross."

"Let's get you something to drink, get that taste out of your mouth." Luna slung her arms around both boys' shoulders and hollered back to Angie, "You coming?"

Angie jogged to catch up. Why had she resisted Luna's inclusion in her life? She fit in seamlessly, simultaneously teasing and encouraging Oliver. It was like she'd always been there.

CHAPTER THIRTEEN

Sunday, September 13

Luna stood in the open door holding a bouquet of lilies, then kissed Angie on the cheek as she handed her the flowers.

"Come in." Angie stepped back, giving Luna room to enter the house.

Luna stopped on the other side of the threshold and stuffed her hands in her pockets. Even though they'd enjoyed a pleasant outing together the day before, Luna was unsure where she fit.

"Let me put these in water, then we can go." Angie headed toward the kitchen, and Luna remained behind.

Oliver ripped around the corner and caught Luna with a flying tackle. She caught him midair, drew him into a stumbling hug, and swung him around before standing him back on his feet. "Hey there."

"Mom didn't tell me you were coming over." The excitement on Oliver's face—he vibrated with it—made Luna smile.

"I'm not really, we're on our way out."

Oliver's excitement faded. "Where are you going?" Oliver's tone fluctuated between pouting child and overprotective parent.

Luna regarded him seriously, resisting the smile that threatened to surface. "Friends of mine are having an anniversary party. They've been together for fifteen years."

Oliver's eyes grew big. "Fifteen years? They must be really old."

Luna laughed. From a ten-year-old perspective, everyone was old.

"Hate to break it to you, champ, but they're not that much older than me."

"Really? How old are you?"

"Thirty-three." Recently Luna had realized how much her friends shared, and she wanted what they had. They'd committed to each other while still in college and had managed to keep the promise through the years. While Luna was out chasing skirts, they were chasing their children around a cramped apartment.

Oliver looked awed. "You're like three of me plus some."

"You say that like I'm ancient." Luna didn't feel old prior to this conversation, but Oliver's assessment was not flattering.

"You're older than Mom."

"How old is she?" Angie had mentioned a ten-year reunion, so that put her below thirty.

"Twenty-seven."

"Really?" Luna was shocked. That meant Angie was seventeen when she had Oliver. Luna had carefully avoided the subject of Oliver's origins because she wasn't ready to pit herself against an ex-lover, one Angie deemed worthy of helping to create a child. With her head-in-the-sand approach, she'd missed out on learning about what must have been a very difficult time for Angie. She felt like an ass.

"Really." Angie joined their conversation. "Are you ready?"

"Sure." Luna held the door open.

"You girls have a good time." Jack stepped into the living room wearing a plaid skirt and combat boots, a dish towel tucked into the waist. "Oliver and I are going to make brownies."

Angie stopped halfway through the door and turned toward her father. She gave him a hard look and said, "Just make sure you follow the recipe exactly."

"No worries, Angie." Jack chuckled. "We'll do just that."

Angie nodded and walked out of the house. A few moments later, they were inside Luna's car and rolling out of the driveway.

"I hate when he does that." Angie blew out a frustrated sigh.

"What?" As far as Luna could tell, Angie was lucky to have a loving and supportive father. Granted, he was a bit eccentric, but he loved Angie and Oliver and, really, wasn't that enough?

"Makes jokes about teaching Oliver inappropriate things."

"Huh?" Luna was even more confused now.

"Think about it, Luna. What's the special ingredient sometimes added to brownies?"

Special ingredient? More than once Luna had brownies made with marijuana at parties. "Are you talking about pot? He wouldn't do that, would he?"

"No, I don't think so, but he would torment me about it. He likes to watch me squirm."

"That's crappy." Luna turned onto the freeway on-ramp. Normally she tried to stick with surface streets, but I-205 was the fastest way to Nan and Vi's house.

"He really isn't being mean, he's just teasing." Angie rested her hand on Luna's thigh, a distraction that probably wasn't safe at freeway speeds, but Luna wasn't about to stop her. "I think it hurts his feelings that I constantly bring it up, so it's a defense mechanism."

"Maybe, but it's still crappy."

"I owe my father a lot. I should cut him some slack."

Luna was intrigued. What had Jack done beyond the normal things a father does for his child? "Like what?"

Angie stared out the window. Eventually she said, "He made a lot of mistakes when I was younger, and I'm still working through all that, but he stayed. And he tried." After a brief pause, Angie said. "He was there when my mom left, and he was there when I had Oliver. That's worth a lot."

Normally a ten-and-two driver, Luna grasped Angie's hand and gently squeezed it. "You're right, that is worth a lot." She wanted Angie to tell her everything, but had learned that Angie didn't respond well when asked to reveal more than she was willing to share. She doled out secrets in sparing bits and pieces, and Luna treasured every one.

"I was so scared. I knew *nothing* about having a baby."

Luna kept her eyes carefully on the road. She didn't want to crowd Angie, and the moment felt too precious to intrude by staring. "You're a great mom."

"Thanks." Angie turned her face toward Luna, a small smile on her lips. "I've spent too much time talking to the assistant principal at Oliver's school to agree, but it's still sweet of you to say."

"I got into trouble all the time as a kid, didn't change that my mom was great." Luna's mom had ruled their home with equal parts loving embrace and iron fist. When guidance didn't work, she'd force Luna back onto the right track. So far Luna had witnessed Angie do the same with Oliver. "You were really young when he was born. You had every right to be scared."

"I was seventeen and so stupid."

"Do you ever see him?" Luna took the off-ramp. They were almost to Nan and Vi's.

"Who? Oliver's father? No." Angie's answer was succinct, her tone distant.

"Why not?" Luna knew she shouldn't ask, but couldn't help herself.

"He doesn't know."

"Doesn't know…" Luna let the thought roll around in her head. What possible reason could Angie have to hide something like a baby? And how had she managed it? "How?"

"It was one time, and when I found out I was pregnant, I left school." The blood drained from Angie's face, like she'd admitted more than she intended.

"You didn't graduate?" The concept was completely foreign to Luna. Above all else, Angela Rinaldi insisted on education. Dropping out would have been unforgivable.

"No, I went to work full time at The Cadillac and tried not to think about the catastrophe my life had turned into."

Luna gripped the steering wheel. "And you never went back?"

"I took the GED a few years ago and got my high-school diploma."

"Well, that's good, right?" Luna tried to imagine her own life if she hadn't earned her degrees. She *might* have been able to gain an apprenticeship without her master's, but the odds of doing so without her bachelor's were very slim. Not to mention the experience she gained while in school. Some of her best memories came from that time in her life. Angie had suffered a tremendous loss.

"Yeah, I'm taking classes from PCC now."

"How do you fit that in?" Between Oliver, work, and the time Angie spent with her, Angie had a tight schedule.

Angie shrugged. "It's all online, so it's flexible."

They neared their destination and Luna pointed to a house with cars lining the driveway. "Here we are." She parked and glanced into the rearview mirror. "Perez and Tori are just pulling in behind us."

As she opened the door and started to climb out, Angie put her hand on her arm and asked her to wait. "How do you feel about sleeping with a high school dropout?"

Eventually Luna hoped she would get used to Angie's take-no-prisoners style of asking questions. The woman did not hesitate when she wanted to know something.

Luna pulled Angie to her for a brief, proprietary kiss. She gripped the back of Angie's head and held her, meeting her gaze solidly. "It feels pretty damn awesome to be with you. The rest is just details."

"You have a master's."

"Yes."

"I have a GED."

"And a beautiful son." Luna had to bring Angie back to the most important part of her life. After all, everything came at a price. "Tell me who wins in that contest?"

"When you put it like that..." Angie kissed her again, lingering longer than considered decent in public. "How do you do that?" She breathed the question into Luna's lips.

"What?"

"Always say the right thing?"

A sharp banging on the hood of her car drew them out of the moment. "You two coming in, or are you going to make out on the street all night?" Perez teased.

Luna pressed her lips to Angie's one last time. Even though she recognized the prudence in disengaging, she'd be damned if she'd let Perez taunt her into aborting her favorite activity prematurely. She rested her forehead against Angie's. "Ready?"

"As I'll ever be." Angie's warm breath puffed across Luna's face and she debated abandoning the party before they even went in. She'd much prefer to have Angie alone and naked than clothed and surrounded by people.

"We need to let go long enough to get out of the car."

"On three?" Angie did the count and they exited the car giggling. Perez and Tori leaned against Perez's car, holding hands and sharing the occasional kiss. They looked more serious than Perez had ever indicated to Luna.

"Is that your car?" Angie sounded disbelieving, and her eyes were open wider than Luna remembered seeing. Granted, Perez drove a nice car, but it really didn't deserve that kind of response.

Perez slipped her sunglasses over her eyes and struck a pose in front of the Audi roadster. "You like?"

"She's your apprentice, right?" Angie asked Luna.

"Right."

"So why is her car nicer than yours?" Angie looked pointedly from Perez's car to Luna's and back again.

"Luna puts her money in the bank." Perez shrugged. "She's practical, whereas I'm still young enough to worry about important things like having a sexy car."

That wasn't the only reason Luna drove the fifteen-year-old Camry, and Perez knew it. Luna was grateful for the attempted smoke screen, but she was at the point of full disclosure with Angie, even if the revelation included emotionally difficult baggage. "It was my mom's car."

Angie's eyes softened and she focused on Luna. "I love it," she said softly.

"Thanks." Luna forgot about Perez, Tori, and the entire damn party. She gazed into Angie's eyes and surrendered her heart completely.

❖

The anniversary party was more intimate than Angie expected. Rather than a lot of people, finger foods, and drinks, there were a few couples, a catered dinner, and mellow music. The only negative so far was Ruby. She sat directly across from Luna, and every time Angie glanced in her direction, Ruby shot icicle glares at her. It was growing tedious.

"Angie." Vi had cornered Angie as she looked over family photos on the wall in the living room. "How did you meet Luna?"

Angie sipped her wine and evaluated Vi. Was she asking because she wanted to know or because she was close to Ruby and was looking for an opportunity to slam Angie as the treacherous other woman?

"Luna did Tori's tattoo. I went along for moral support. We met Luna, Perez, and Ruby all at the same time." Angie glanced at Tori, who was seated on the sofa and studiously focused on Perez.

"And then what? Did you guys hook up then?"

"God, no. Luna was with Ruby. I wasn't willing to go there." Angie mentally squirmed under Vi's scrutiny. What was she up to?

"Really?" Vi looked confused. "But those two never really *dated*. They were more just friends with benefits."

Wow. So Luna had been telling the truth about the nature of her relationship with Ruby. It was just so at odds with Ruby's display of possessiveness outside Coraggio that first night. That had stayed with Angie long after Luna left Ruby. Despite Luna's assurances that their relationship was purely sexual, Ruby clearly had designs on Luna's future. Discovering that her plans would never reach fruition must have been a bitter pill. Ruby's animosity bothered Angie a little less when she kept that hard truth in mind. She wouldn't have wanted to trade roles with Ruby.

"That's what Luna said, but I wasn't taking any chances." Angie studied Luna, who was obviously listening but avoiding involvement in the conversation.

"Well, you two found each other, and that's all that matters," Vi stated. She looked proud.

"Was it love at first sight?" Nan joined them, her eyes dreamy. "That's how it was for me and Vi."

"I don't know about that." Angie laughed and hoped she sounded relaxed, though she wanted to strangle something. "But she definitely got my attention." She didn't want to offend her hosts, but the subject matter really needed to change soon.

"What about you, Luna?"

Luna stepped closer and placed her hand reassuringly on Angie's low back. She moved her fingers in a light semicircle as she answered, her tone serious, "Love is defined in the long term, not in the moment."

"Ah, I disagree," said Perez. "I fall in love every time the Victoria's Secret catalog arrives."

Tori smacked Perez's shoulder. "I'd be offended, but the same thing happens to me."

"Well, I fell in love in an instant, and it's only grown stronger with time." Vi lifted her wineglass, raising her voice to encompass the room. "A toast to my beautiful wife. Thank you for fifteen wonderful years."

Fifteen years was a lifetime to Angie. She tried to picture that far in the future and came up with a blank. Oliver would be twenty-five years old, but where would she be? Who would she be with? Was she building the foundation for something real, something lasting, with Luna? The vision was there, just out of reach. She could see the form, but the details were missing.

She wanted Luna, but what if Luna changed her mind? What if she let herself really *love* Luna, then Luna decided she wasn't worth it? That a relationship with a single mom and a difficult potential stepchild was just too much work? Her hesitation wasn't just about Oliver, she realized. It was about not getting hurt.

Angie drank the toast and hoped her hosts' focus would remain on one another. She didn't want to discuss her first meeting with Luna any more. And she really didn't want to debate the plausibility of love at first sight. The origins of her relationship with Luna were suspect at best. They would not stand up to scrutiny since Luna had pursued Angie while still committed to Ruby. Nothing more than a kiss had happened until after they split, but the intention had been there. Angie hadn't reflected a lot on how their actions affected Ruby, but with the woman in the same room, it was difficult to not face her guilt. She hated that she'd split up a long-term couple, no matter the context of their relationship.

When they finished drinking the toast, Nan suggested they take the party to the back patio. "It's sure to be one of the last decent nights this year. We should take advantage of it."

The yard was alight with several pathway illuminators, and the pond glowed from within. Tiny outdoor speakers filled the otherwise quiet night with the smooth, silky singing of Ella Fitzgerald. These women had the kind of toys that Angie was on the verge of giving up dreaming about. She relaxed as the music surrounded her.

"Dance with me." Luna pulled her close, one hand possessively low on her back, the other entwined with one of Angie's and tucked between them. Angie looped her free arm around Luna's shoulder, playing with the loose, wild curls falling over her back. "Thanks for coming with me tonight." Luna's voice was intimately quiet and low, and her lips tickled Angie's ear.

"My pleasure." Angie stretched her body against Luna's, luxuriating in her embrace.

"I'm sorry about Ruby." Luna slowed their movement until they were barely swaying, her forehead resting against Angie's, her eyes closed.

"It's okay," Angie whispered, "a little awkward, but okay."

Luna gathered her closer. "I must have been really good in a past life to deserve you."

"A past life?" Angie thought just the opposite. She figured Luna was her compensation for all the crap life had piled on her until this point.

"Yeah, God knows I haven't been anything but bad this time around." Luna smiled gently and brushed her lips over Angie's. Luna approached her with such reverence, Angie felt worshipped. At times the intensity frightened her.

"You feel great from here." It was the first time they'd danced together and Angie wanted the moment to last forever. Luna's arms felt perfect around her, safe and loving, like a promise begging to be fulfilled.

They rocked together without speaking as the music transitioned from Ella to the lower, sultrier voice of Diana Krall. Angie cracked open one eye and peeked at the other women. Tori and Perez were dancing also, talking and smiling as they moved slowly to the music. Did Tori feel as overwhelmed by Perez as she did by Luna? She was a tidal wave washing over and pulling Angie under, and God help her, she didn't want to break the surface.

Angie closed her eye and tightened her grip on the curls at the base of Luna's neck. She loved this woman. She was almost certain of it, and the thought terrified her. Angie nuzzled into Luna's neck and let the sweet smell of sweat on her skin, the low pulse of electricity between them lull her thoughts away. In that moment, nothing mattered but the woman in her arms and the skin beneath her lips.

"You need to take me home soon, or I'll forget we're surrounded by your friends."

Luna moaned at her breathless proclamation. She released Angie's hand and moved her other one to rest on Angie's ass. She grasped Angie, pulling her tight against her, rocking her pelvis subtly into Angie as she kneaded and massaged the fleshy swell.

"Let's go then," Luna whispered into her ear.

They waited for the song to finish, then forced their bodies apart. The separation bordered on painful.

Chapter Fourteen

"I can't believe you two are ducking out so early." Tori pushed her way into the small bathroom behind Angie and shut the door. "If I have to stay, so should you."

Angie checked her face in the mirror. Rather than try to repair the damage slow dancing—and kissing—with Luna had caused, she simply handed her makeup to Tori and said, "Fix it?"

"You're helpless." Tori's tone and smile said she loved her role as makeup artist for Angie, despite her attempt to sound frustrated.

"And you're sweet." Angie focused on the wall behind Tori as she reapplied her eyeliner and mascara. That experience unnerved Angie and it took all her willpower not to squirm away from the brush approaching her eyes. "I'd stay and entertain you, but I'd rather take Luna home and fuck her silly."

"Well, when you put it that way—pucker—" Tori made a kissy face at Angie and held up Angie's lip gloss. "I wouldn't stay either if that offer was on the table," she said as she applied the gloss Angie had purchased based on the promise that her lips would remain kissably wet all evening. So far that had proved to be a lie.

"You are not allowed to have sex with Luna." Angie closed her eyes as Tori freshened her eye shadow.

"Funny. Keep your eyes closed. A little powder and you're all done." Tori ran the soft-bristle brush over Angie's cheeks. "I meant if sex in general was on the table I'd be out of here."

"You aren't sleeping with Perez?"

"Of course I am, but that's not an option tonight. She's got her period and that's not my kind of thrill."

"Bummer," Angie said.

"Indeed." Tori turned Angie toward the mirror. "How'd I do?"

"Perfect, thank you." Her makeup always looked a hundred times better when Tori did it. Why was that?

"How'd things go yesterday with Oliver?" Tori turned her talents onto her own face and Angie propped herself against the counter to wait for her to finish.

"It was good." Angie hadn't had a chance to discuss their outing with Tori last night at work. It had been too busy for even their normal playful banter between tables. "Oliver is very fond of Luna."

"And she likes him, too, right?"

"She's like a giant kid. She chased him around other people between rides, and she went on all the rides with him and Josh that normal adults avoid."

"Sounds like a success."

"Yeah, the boys were really upset when we had to leave because Luna had an appointment with a client, but it was a good lesson in responsibility for Oliver." When Angie had to cut a day short to go to work, Oliver treated her like he was being abandoned, but with Luna he had listened to her explanation about the importance of meeting obligations, then left without further protest.

"Did he throw a fit?"

"Amazingly, no. He just followed Luna, looking like a rejected puppy. It was sad and cute at the same time."

"What time are you expected home tonight?"

"I told Jack not to wait up." That had been a difficult request for Angie. She didn't plan to be gone all night, but also didn't want to rush home from her date. She'd had precious few official dates since Oliver was born and wanted to savor every moment, especially with Luna.

Tori finished with her makeup and opened the bathroom door. "We should get back." She gestured for Angie to exit first.

Angie hugged Tori gently before passing. "Thanks for being such a good friend."

"Back atcha, babe." Tori released the hug and gave her an exaggerated wink. "Now go find your woman."

❖

Nan held out the bottle of wine, an offer to refill Luna's glass.

"No, thanks." Luna covered the top with her hand.

"Time was that 'No, thanks' would have been followed by 'Where's the Jack?'" Nan topped off her own drink.

"Yeah, but now I want to remember the things I do the next day."

"Angie seems nice." Nan sipped her wine and peered at Luna over the top of her glass.

"She is."

"Really nice."

"What's your point, Nan?" Luna was getting antsy. She just wanted to collect Angie and go home, not have a conversation with Nan that required a decoder ring.

"You think she's the *one*?" Nan played with the commitment ring on her left hand.

"I don't know." If Luna was being completely honest, she definitely thought Angie was the one, but that didn't mean she was ready to say it aloud, certainly not before she discussed it with Angie. She shrugged. "Maybe."

"You two are good together."

As much as Luna appreciated Nan's endorsement, tonight was the first time she'd even met Angie. "What makes you say that?"

"You two remind me of me and Vi fifteen years ago," Nan said.

Luna nodded. Her friends had been ridiculously in love back then, to the exclusion of all those around them. Luna had been simultaneously annoyed and jealous.

"Sorry about Ruby." Nan patted her shoulder. "It hasn't been too awkward here tonight, has it?"

"It's been fine, except maybe when Vi gave Angie the third degree."

Nan chuckled. "She's incorrigible, really."

"Angie did all right, though." Luna had been proud of the way Angie navigated Vi's endless stream of questions.

"We considered uninviting one of you." Nan gave her a wicked smile. "But we love you both and decided you could just deal. Our anniversary, our rules."

"Makes sense."

"So where is Angie now?" Nan scanned the room.

"She ducked into the bathroom with Tori." It was a ritual that Luna would never understand, the need for girls to go to the restroom together. There were certain things she just didn't want an audience for.

"After that dance, I figured you'd be gone by now."

"That's the plan." Luna drained her wineglass and sat it on the kitchen counter. "I'll go grab our jackets from the bedroom. Hopefully Angie will be ready by the time I come back."

Nan hugged Luna. "Let's get together for dinner soon, just the four of us."

"Sounds good." Somehow the thought of spending time with a legitimate long-time couple made a future with Angie seem more real.

Luna had her hand on the doorknob before she realized that Ruby had followed her to the bedroom. She entered the room with Ruby close behind her. She didn't like being isolated with her ex-lover, but they were grownups. Surely they could be in the same room together without disastrous results.

Ruby closed the door behind her and stood with her back against it, effectively blocking Luna's only point of egress.

"What do you want, Ruby?" Luna sounded more irritated than she intended.

"To talk, lover. I've missed you." Ruby followed Luna's movements with her eyes, and the thorough inspection made Luna feel a little dirty.

"You don't get to call me that anymore," Luna answered softly. She didn't want an ugly confrontation. She found Angie's jacket and headed toward the door. Hopefully Ruby would move out of the way.

"Why not? I've called you that forever." Ruby didn't step aside for Luna to pass.

"Angie wouldn't like it." Luna waited a few minutes. "I need out, Ruby."

Ruby took a step forward. "You want me to move?"

Luna shifted to the side and edged against the wall to let Ruby pass. She pointed at the door. "Angie's waiting."

Ruby stepped closer to Luna, trapping her. "I just want to talk."

Luna dropped Angie's jacket and put her hands up. How the hell had she gotten into this position? She blinked, hoping Ruby would prove a bad hallucination and would disappear if she cleared her vision. No such luck. "What could we possibly have to talk about?"

Ruby relaxed and eased away, her arms no longer boxing Luna in. "About us. I don't like where we left things."

"Neither do I, but nothing has changed." Luna couldn't believe it. Now, when she should be home with Angie's clothes halfway off, she was having *this* conversation with Ruby.

"We were good together." Ruby crossed her arms.

"We were convenient together." Luna didn't want to hurt Ruby, but she wanted to be clear. Ruby had a habit of hearing only what she wanted. "Nothing more."

"I wanted more." Ruby picked up Angie's jacket and smoothed the wrinkles. "I still want more."

"It never would have worked." Luna took Angie's coat. Angie wouldn't want Ruby caring for it. "I need someone who needs me, someone who thinks about more than just herself." Luna wondered about her statement. She wasn't sure Angie would ever admit to needing her, but Luna was determined to prove she could.

"I needed you." Tears threatened to spill from Ruby's perfectly made-up eyes. Luna hoped she could hold it together.

"No, Ruby, you didn't." Luna spoke softly. She would tell the truth, but she really didn't want to be cruel. "You needed to get off. Occasionally you needed to be held afterward, but you never needed *me.*"

"I could tell her that you're still in love with me." Ruby's eyes narrowed. "She'd believe me, you know. She's about two steps away from running as it is."

"That's not true." Of course it was true. Angie told her all the time. *Wait. I don't know when I can see you again. Not yet.* Luna felt as if her life was on perpetual hold waiting for Angie to decide she was worthy. Still, she'd rather wait for Angie's approval, her love, than to settle for second-best with Ruby. "Even if she left right now, we'd still be over. You need to understand that."

"Luna, be reasonable. Since when do you want children?"

"For a while." Luna looked away. She couldn't bear the confusion and underlying sadness in Ruby's eyes.

"She'll string you along and then she'll leave you." Ruby took half a step toward Luna. "She doesn't want, let alone *need* you."

"Yes, she does." Even if she wouldn't admit it, Luna knew the truth. She knew from years of watching her mom struggle. Angie needed her. No doubt about it.

"You sound so sure."

"I am." Luna hoped she sounded more confident than she felt. Just because she knew Angie needed her didn't mean Angie would ever tell her.

"I think I'll ask her for myself." Ruby looked toward the partially open door. "You planning to join us?"

Angie stepped in, closed the door behind her, and turned the lock. "Just in case." She gave Ruby a half-smile.

"How long have you been there?" Luna braced herself. She hadn't even heard the door open, let alone been aware of Angie's presence.

"Too long? Not long enough? Depends on who you'd ask." Angie forced herself to breathe slowly, evenly. Finding Luna shut in a bedroom with her ex-lover wasn't the end of the world, but Angie could think of about five thousand other things she'd rather be doing at the moment. "I was looking for you."

Luna held up her jacket. "I came to get this."

"I see." Angie reached for it. "Thank you." She allowed Luna to help her into the light fall coat and used the time to order her thoughts. They flitted from one to the next without ever grabbing hold of one. *Ruby loved Luna. Luna thought Angie needed her. Ruby would always be there, waiting for her to fail. Luna wanted children.* She'd need time to put them in order, make them make sense. "Do you need a few more minutes? I can wait in the car."

"We're done here." Luna took a step in her direction and Angie mentally sighed in relief. She didn't want to leave Luna alone with Ruby for even a second longer.

"No, we're not." Ruby reclined against the wall. Her body language said she was relaxed, but her eyes were all predator and focused on

Angie. "You don't appreciate her. You'll tie her down and wear her spirit until she can't take it anymore, then she'll leave. Why don't you save all the suffering and let her go now?"

"You don't know me." Angie clung to her shredded self-control. "Don't act like you do."

"I know *exactly* who you are. A little know-nothing, have-nothing fuck-up who couldn't keep her legs closed in high school, then couldn't keep her hands off my woman." Ruby pushed herself close to Angie. "You're a nobody. I know it. You know it. Eventually Luna will know it."

Ruby's words, combined with the overpowering scent of expensive perfume and top-shelf gin, made Angie's head spin. She reacted before she could think. The loud slap of her palm against Ruby's cheek shocked both of them to silence.

Ruby cupped her face protectively, her breath ragged. "You bitch."

Angie could hear Ruby's voice behind her as Luna guided her from the room and closed the door.

❖

"That was awkward." Luna pulled to a stop in Angie's driveway. They'd sat in uncomfortable silence the entire ride to her house. Luna was desperate to break the tension, to figure out how Angie was reacting.

"To say the least." Angie gave her a weak smile.

Luna laced her fingers with Angie's. The contact soothed her. "I'm sorry about Ruby."

Angie shrugged. "It's not your fault."

It *felt* like it was her fault. She knew how nasty Ruby could get, yet she hadn't shielded Angie, hadn't protected her. "I wish I'd done something to stop her."

"She uses the truth as a weapon, doesn't she?" Angie sounded sad, like a woman with regrets. Her tone made Luna nervous.

"Nothing she said was true, Angie. Nothing."

"Mmm."

Luna didn't know how to convince Angie. Ruby had been lashing out, plain and simple. The woman did not fight fair.

"I should walk you to the door."

Angie shook her head and pulled her hand free. "You don't need to."

"Of course I do."

Angie stared out the window and didn't respond.

"If you factor out the fifteen minutes with Ruby, tonight was really fun." Luna squeezed Angie's hand. "Let's do something with Oliver again next weekend. We can take him to the movies. Or maybe hiking. I know some great trails."

Angie pulled away. "I don't think so."

Luna pushed her hands through her hair. It was tangled at the bottom. Angie frustrated her so much. When they were alone together, Angie was so passionate, so *present*. Luna couldn't get enough. When the rest of the world encroached, Angie fled. Luna wanted more. She wanted to be a part of the family that Angie guarded so fiercely. She wanted to *matter*. One thing was certain, she couldn't continue on the emotional scraps that Angie doled out.

"Angie, what are we doing? You and I? I need to be more than just an afterthought in your life. I want to build something real together." Luna held her breath and waited.

Angie looked her in the eye for the first time since leaving the party. "I don't think we should see each other again."

"What?" This was not the outcome Luna was hoping for.

"Ruby was right about a few things." Angie looked at her feet, then up again to meet Luna's gaze. "I can't let you break my heart."

"I won't." Luna shook her head once, hard and with certainty. "That's simply not an option."

"You will. Eventually." Angie gripped the door handle and cracked the door open. The dome light came on. "It's easier this way."

"You've been looking for a reason to run away from this, from *us*," Luna gestured between them, "since the beginning. Please, Angie, I need you to find a reason to run *to* us." Angie had this wall of eerie calm around her and Luna didn't know how to crack it.

"Why?" Angie's eyes glistened in the dim light, her bottom lip trembled slightly.

"Because I love you." The words slipped out. Very true, but very unintended. Luna straightened her shoulders and waited.

"I wish that was enough, Luna." She climbed out of the car and walked away into the night, leaving Luna behind. Tight bands of loss circled Luna's chest and the weight was crushing.

If love wasn't enough, what was?

CHAPTER FIFTEEN

Tuesday, September 22

"It's perfect." Perez spread her arms and spun in a circle.

Luna inspected the warehouse with slightly less enthusiasm. It wasn't that she didn't like it. She did. But since Angie told her they shared no future together, her life had been covered in cellophane. Her emotions were still there, she just couldn't quite touch them. Still, Perez's hard work and excitement deserved acknowledgment.

"It's great."

"Great?" Perez shook Luna's arm. "It's way better than great, Luna."

The industrial building had a spacious, open floor plan that could easily be partitioned off. Luna mentally placed the reception area and eight private rooms. That left more than half of the available space unaccounted for. "It's more space than we need."

"That's true." Perez pulled the folded property listing from her pocket and smoothed the creases. "But it costs less than other places with half the room."

Luna didn't understand why. The neighborhood wasn't great, but it wasn't the worst in Portland. Hell, the crime rate was probably a little lower than it was at their current location. The building didn't appear to have any major structural problems, but an inspection would determine that for sure. "Why is that?"

Perez shrugged and looked at the real-estate agent, a cheerful woman named Jean.

"The current owner is very eager to sell. Some unfortunate personal events make quick turnover more important than a big sale."

Luna tried to remember the numbers that Perez had laid out in the car. She'd outlined in detail the asking price, required deposit, and projected monthly payment. It had turned into a jumble of numbers in Luna's head. "Tell me the numbers again."

Perez broke it down for her. Luna's income alone would cover the mortgage, but not much else. Between her and Perez, however, a piece of cake.

"And this is the place you want?" Luna was in no shape to make major decisions, and maybe she was making a serious mistake leaving it all to Perez to decide. She was willing to find out.

"Hell, yes." Perez nodded, momentarily abandoning her normal cool.

Luna looked around again, trying to take it all in, force order into the chaos in her head. She sighed. "I don't know, Perez."

Perez stared at her, then turned to Jean. "Can you give us a minute?"

"Take your time." Jean smiled. "I'm heading across the street for a cup of coffee."

Perez waited until the door closed behind her, then said, "It's been a week. Have you talked to her at all?"

Luna hated how absolutely dependent on Angie she'd become so quickly. More than that, she hated how obvious it was to others. She was a wreck and Angie could fix it with one word.

"She won't return my calls." Luna had phoned nonstop for the first couple of days. When she realized how desperate her actions were, she forced herself to slow the pace. Now she held herself at a strict limit of ten messages per day. She was pathetic and she didn't care.

"Have you seen her?" If Perez was annoyed at suspending their business dealings, it didn't show. She was all concerned friend the moment Jean left the building.

"No." Unless she counted watching Angie walk past on her way to and from work. She'd stared longingly from behind her window, willing Angie to open the door and come in. Since Angie didn't so much as look in her direction, Luna didn't consider those non-encounters worth mentioning.

"Why don't you go to her house?"

Luna looked twice to make sure Perez was serious. She was. "Because she'll call the police. You gonna bail me out?" Luna was only half joking.

"Her dad won't let her do that."

Luna liked Jack, and he seemed to like her. But most likely his affection didn't extend far enough to shift his loyalty from Angie to her. At least she hoped not. It would break Angie's heart. "I'm not willing to take the chance."

"Really? Then you need to forget about Angie and move on."

"What the fuck, Perez?" Where did the supportive friend go?

"If you don't grow some balls, and soon, you don't stand a chance. It's best if you let her go now if that's the case."

"That's harsh."

"It's the truth. Either do something or get over it. This whole walking-around-in-a-daze thing needs to end."

"I'm only allowed to be hurt on your timetable, is that it?" Luna bordered on shouting.

Perez put her hands on her hips. "Stop being such an asshole and go see Angie. Beg if you have to, I don't care. Make her see how much she means to you."

"It's not that simple."

"It is. Exactly that simple."

Luna paused. When Perez said it, it sounded so easy. But it wouldn't be. "I already tried that and it didn't work."

"If you love her, *really* love her, then you'll try harder." Perez spoke like Luna was a particularly slow learner.

Jean returned with a carrier full of coffee. "Hope I'm not too soon." She handed a cup to Perez and one to Luna.

Perez smiled at Luna, her eyes soft and encouraging, before turning her attention to Jean. "Just in time, I'd say."

"Did you make a decision?" Jean smiled like the eternally optimistic salesperson that she was.

"I don't know." Perez looked pointedly at Luna. "Did we?"

Luna considered what they'd discussed and wondered how much of Perez's message was just about Angie and how much had to do with Coraggio as well. She had too much up in the air. She needed to decide about something, even it was just surrendering the decision-making to Perez. After all, this move meant just as much, if not more, to Perez as it did to her.

Luna sipped her coffee and nodded. "Let's do it."

❖

Angie rubbed her eyes and reread the paragraph for the third time. She inserted her bookmark and considered officially giving up on accounting for the day. The receptionist smiled at her in an I-take-too-much-Zoloft kind of way, and Angie doubted her decision to let Oliver talk to the therapist alone. She genuinely believed he would open up easier if she wasn't present, but at the same time she didn't want him emerging from the inner workings of Dunloff, Knopp, and Lee in an overmedicated stupor. Oliver was entitled to the full measure of his emotions—providing he didn't force them on others—rather than the mellow middle ground that mood-enhancing drugs produced.

She was overreacting, but knowing it didn't stop her. Oliver was her only child. She was supposed to protect him. With that overactive mama-bear instinct also came some seriously overactive paranoid delusions.

Angie sighed and reopened the book. The practical side of her personality insisted that she use her time in the waiting room wisely. Simply sitting there and imagining the worse wouldn't do any good. She gave up trying to understand what she was reading and compromised by moving her eyes over the words while allowing her mind to wander. This imperfect compromise was the best she could come up with.

"I'm ready, Mom." Oliver ran over to Angie, moving on overdrive, like always.

Dr. Knopp followed. "Can I speak to you for a few minutes, Ms. Dressen?" She gestured for Angie to enter her office. "Oliver will be fine here, won't you, Oliver?"

"Yeah, go ahead, Mom. I'll be okay."

Angie smiled at Oliver, not at all sure he would. She followed the doctor through the door.

"Please, have a seat." Dr. Knopp seated herself behind the desk.

Angie was glad. If she'd chosen the traditional therapist chair and client on the couch layout, Angie would have been uncomfortable enough to consider leaving.

Angie waited, but Dr. Knopp didn't speak again. Was this a cheap parlor trick that therapists used to see how long the other person could go without filling the silence? Angie's threshold proved to be fairly low. She didn't feel like dicking around when it came to Oliver's well-being. "What did you need?"

"I'm not sure what your concerns are with Oliver?" Dr. Knopp raised her eyebrow, inviting Angie to fill in the blanks. This time Angie didn't. Dr. Knopp continued. "But I can assure you that Oliver is a normal prepubescent boy."

Angie relented. She needed to know if she should expect a repeat performance or if Oliver's uncharacteristic display that day had been a one-off. "He got into a fight at school where he held down a smaller boy and drew a tattoo of an angel on his arm."

"And you want to know if he'll do anything like that again."

"Yes." God, Angie hoped not.

"Of course I can't predict the future, but I don't see evidence of a violent nature in Oliver." Dr. Knopp consulted her notes. "He knows that was wrong and is genuinely remorseful."

"Well, that's good, right?" Angie dared to hope.

"It is, yes."

"Do you think he needs to come back?" Angie held her breath while she waited for the answer.

"Not for that issue, no." Dr. Knopp left the sentence up in the air, like she had more to say even though she'd technically finished the answer.

"But?" Angie hated what came after *but*. It was never good. She forced herself to breathe.

"He has some issues to work through, just like any other child his age."

"I'll think about it." Angie didn't want to deny Oliver help if he genuinely needed it, but didn't want to condemn him to a life of therapy before she'd had a chance to truly drive him to require it. She stood. "If there's nothing else?"

"That covers it, Ms. Dressen."

Angie made a hasty retreat before Dr. Knopp could think of another reason to detain her. Strangely, the experience felt reminiscent of being called to the assistant principal's office. She didn't slow on her way through the reception area. "Come on, son, time to go."

Oliver scrambled to catch up. "Can we stop for ice cream on the way home?"

"Why not?" As far as Angie was concerned, a clean bill of mental health was reason to celebrate.

They pulled through the local Dairy Queen on the way home, a vanilla cone for Angie, a chocolate swirl for Oliver.

"Mom…" Oliver caught Angie's eyes in the rearview mirror. He still wasn't old enough to sit in the front seat because of the airbag. That was a milestone he was looking forward to and Angie was dreading. It would be one more irrefutable sign that her little boy was growing up.

"Yes, baby?" Angie tensed and waited for Oliver to throw a fit about being too big to be called *baby*. When it didn't come, she smiled. Could she get away with tousling his hair, too? She'd never find out because she was driving, but the thought made her feel good.

"I miss Luna." He took a hasty lick of ice cream, catching a potential drip before it could fall. "When is she coming over again?"

Angie's heart clenched. This was exactly why she hadn't wanted Luna to get involved with Oliver. She *knew* when he got attached, something would go wrong and she'd be left to protect him from a broken heart. As it was, she wasn't doing a very good job keeping her own heart safe, so how could she hope to do so for Oliver?

"I know you do, son." Angie opted for frank, if not all-inclusive, honesty. "So do I."

"Then make her come see us."

"It doesn't work that way."

"You're the mom. That means you're in charge."

"Yes, but I'm not Luna's mom." In spite of Angie's denial, she knew that one word from her and Luna would be over before she could disconnect the phone call. She wasn't ready. "So that rule doesn't work with her."

"Well, that's dumb."

"I agree." Angie turned into the driveway and pushed the button on her garage-door opener. She was halfway in before she realized Luna was sitting on her doorstep.

"Luna!" Oliver yelled, and jumped out of the car before Angie fully stopped.

Angie parked the car and followed Oliver out of the garage to the front porch. She stood back and let Oliver talk to Luna uninterrupted. Luna stood, hands stuffed in her pockets, and smiled at Angie over the top of Oliver's head. "Hi, Angie."

"Mom got me ice cream. I didn't know you'd be here or I would have brought you some. You can have some of mine if you want." Oliver thrust his melting ice cream into Luna's face.

"Whoa, easy does it, buddy." Luna laughed and took an exaggerated bite of Oliver's ice cream.

"Are you coming in? Grandpa is making pizza tonight. It's way better than takeout, and I got a new video game. You have to play it with me. Come on." Oliver tugged Luna's arm.

"Let me talk to your mom, okay?" Luna's smile was sad, and Angie wanted to send her after Oliver just so they could play video games together and be happy for a few hours. She didn't.

"Oliver, go help Grandpa with dinner." Angie handed her ice cream to Oliver.

"Fine, but you can't let her leave without coming inside first." Oliver pouted, then ran inside yelling, "Grandpa, did you know Luna's here?" The door slammed behind him.

"Luna." Angie ached to take Luna into her arms. It'd been too long since she'd felt her body against hers. "What are you doing here?"

"We need to talk." Luna twisted her hands together.

"Does Jack know you're here?" Angie couldn't imagine her father leaving Luna on the front step if he was aware of her presence.

"He does, but I insisted on waiting here. Didn't want a repeat of Labor Day."

Angie knew she should invite Luna in. It was the only polite thing to do. But she didn't feel like being polite when it would cost her emotional ground. She gestured toward the step where Luna had previously been seated. "Want to sit?"

Luna nodded, her face grim, and settled onto the top step. Angie sat next to her. Neither of them spoke for several minutes.

"You haven't returned my calls." Luna didn't look at Angie. "So I came here instead of leaving another message."

"You shouldn't have." Angie could forget why she didn't want to see Luna if she stayed much longer. "You should go."

"I had to see you." Luna remained seated. "Please, Angie, you have to talk to me."

"No, I don't." Angie sounded like a bitch.

"I love you." Luna said the words like she knew they wouldn't change Angie's mind.

"I know." Words that should mean everything just didn't suffice.

Luna took Angie's hand. "I can't just walk away from you, Angie. I just can't."

"Oliver's been asking about you." Angie couldn't see her way clear to trust Luna. Not with her future, with her heart. It would hurt too much if she was wrong. "This is what I was afraid of."

"Let me come in. I promise I won't disappoint you." Luna regarded Angie, her eyes pleading.

"I want to," Angie whispered, shocked at the admission.

Luna squeezed her hand. "Then do it."

"It's not that simple." Angie closed her eyes and shook her head. "It's never that simple."

"Yes, it is. I love you and I think you love me."

Angie didn't respond.

"Do you?"

Angie blinked, but the movement didn't hold back her tears. She wiped them away before Luna could touch her. "I don't know."

"I do." Luna cupped her cheek. "I *know*. I can see it in your eyes."

Of course Luna could see it. Angie barely had a handle on her emotions. The whole world probably knew. "It's not enough." Angie pulled away from Luna's embrace.

"It can be if you let it." Luna's belief that love conquered all was charmingly naïve. Not that Angie had ever been in love, but she was practical enough to know that it had some very serious limitations.

"This isn't a Broadway musical. This is *my life*." Angie stood, unable to bear the closeness to Luna any longer. "Love isn't worth a damn without trust."

Luna stood and faced her. "Angie, you want me to make impossible promises, to predict the future. I can't. I can just promise to love you."

"But that's just it. No matter how many times you say that, it won't change reality. I don't know how to have faith in love. Yours or mine. We can't build a future on that."

Luna pulled Angie's hand to her chest. "Can we build it on the fact that my heart stops beating just a little every time I see you? Or that it breaks every time I think about how much my mom would have loved you and then I realize she'll never have the chance to even meet you? How about the fact that Oliver makes me want to be a better person so I can be the kind of example he deserves? Or that I don't want to commit horrible acts of violence when you take control of my remote?" Luna brushed her lips against Angie's. "What about the part where you're the person I want to fall asleep and wake up next to? And I can't promise forever, but that's what I want. That's how it feels to me. Please, Angie, we deserve the chance to find out how far we can go."

Luna's plea was impassioned and Angie agreed with every point. She felt the same way, wanted the same things, but she was too afraid to grab it.

"I can't." Angie stopped trying to not cry. It was too late for that. "Everything you said sounds beautiful, but it's impossible. I don't trust love. People say *I do* and a few years later say *I don't*."

"I won't give up, Angie. I love you. Nothing will change that."

Angie left Luna standing on the porch. She couldn't be near her for even a minute longer or her resolve would crumble. Ultimately, she'd regret it if she gave in. She just couldn't let go of the dark fear in her chest. It was the same feeling she had watching woman after woman—starting with her own mother—walk out on her father. She simply couldn't stand the anxious feeling of waiting for Luna to do the same. She already cared too much and refused to get in any deeper. The inevitable loss and pain weren't worth it.

She closed the door and rested her back against the hard surface. Gravity and mental exhaustion worked together and she crumpled to the floor, hugged her knees to her chest, and cried.

"Tell her you're sorry, that you didn't mean any of what you said. Tell her to come back," Oliver yelled, and pointed out the window. "Do it."

Angie forced herself to stop crying. The tears would do no good, and her son needed her. "Oliver, you don't know what you're talking about."

"I know you sent her away after she said she loves you." Oliver glared, his ten-year-old disapproval palpable.

Angie refused to engage in this conversation with Oliver. "I'm going to take a shower." It was odd timing, to say the least. She could smell dinner cooking, but she needed to get clean. She was drowning in emotional residue and the shower would help. It had to.

"Mom, please, you can still fix this."

"Not this time, son."

Angie pulled the bathroom door shut on the conversation, turned the water on, and shed her clothing. As the water ran over her, she knew no amount of body wash and shampoo would erase the fact that her son thought she was an asshole.

Angie agreed.

Chapter Sixteen

Thursday, September 24

Angie moved the clothes in the dryer to her basket and the ones in the washer to the dryer. Even with Jack filling the role of stay-at-home parent, there was still an endless supply of laundry. And dishes. Floors to be vacuumed. Homework to be checked. Windows to be cleaned. For the first time, Angie was grateful. If she was careful, and worked hard, she could avoid thinking about Luna.

A single knock on the kitchen door announced Tori's arrival a half second before she walked into the room. At the same time, "I'm So Tired of Being Alone" came on the radio. All Angie's effort to *not* think about Luna was shot to hell as their first dinner together rushed through her mind.

She grunted and threw the basket, clothes and all, at the wall. It hit with a satisfying smack and bounced off, dumping clothes on the floor.

Tori looked at Angie, the basket, then Angie again. "Is this what I can expect every time you hear Al Green?"

Angie thought about it. Throwing things as a response to music, one of her used-to-be favorite songs, no less, seemed a tad over the top. Strangely, that didn't bother her as much as it probably should have. "Yes. I think so."

"Good to know." Tori helped Angie pick the clothes up, folding as she went. "On the upside, it'll help me develop those catlike reflexes I've been working on."

Angie loved Tori for finding the positive in a seriously unpleasant situation. "I'll try to time it for when you're around."

"You planning to ever get over yourself?" Tori didn't avoid tough questions, and Angie's love dwindled a little because of it.

"Don't be silly." Angie carried the basket to her bedroom. Tori followed.

"You think this is silly?" Tori grabbed a handful of hangers from the closet.

"I think I don't want to talk about it." Angie stuffed a stack of T-shirts into the drawer, but it wasn't nearly as fulfilling as throwing the whole basket had been. She started on her blouses next, with a little more care since she didn't want to shove a hanger through one of them.

"She didn't do anything wrong, Angie."

"I *know* that. This isn't about right or wrong." *It's about self-preservation.* Angie had heard all the arguments. Intellectually, she understood. Really, she did. "I just can't shake the fear of losing Luna. My only option was to give her up before I got too deep."

"You realize how fucking mental that sounds?" Tori looked ready to throw a basket of her own.

"Mental or not, it's how I feel." Angie was tired of talking about it. "Why do you care so much?"

Tori's face softened. "Because I love you." She squeezed Angie's shoulder. "Besides, Luna's miserable. And when she's miserable, Perez is miserable. And then I don't get laid. Your inability to get over it is affecting my sex life in a major way. Seriously not cool."

The only thing Angie heard was "Luna's miserable."

"Is Luna really that bad?" A tiny—minuscule, really—part of her felt good to know that Luna was suffering, too.

"Focus!" Tori clapped her hands together. "The important thing here is that I'm not getting any lovin'. This can't go on."

Angie rubbed her eyes. "I don't know what to do."

"Honey." Tori hugged Angie to her. "I'm sorry."

Tori rocked Angie, her arms a safe haven. Eventually Angie disengaged and resumed putting her blouses on hangers.

"So is this your big plan? Go back into hibernation, hiding like you did before you met Luna?"

"What do you want me to do? Go clubbing every night?"

"How 'bout just once?" Tori stood, too, and grabbed Angie by the shoulders, forcing her to stop pacing the distance from her bed to the closet and back again.

"Nothing's changed, Tori. I still have a ten-year-old son."

"That didn't stop you from finding time for Luna."

"Maybe it should have."

❖

Rain drizzled down, not enough to warrant Angie using her umbrella, but enough to make sure she was completely damp by the time she'd walked two blocks from her house. Fall in Portland was her least favorite season. The days were shorter and the weather unpredictable.

"Summer is officially over." Tori wore an elaborate raincoat and matching boots. It was terribly overcoordinated for the Northwest and a perfect fit for Tori's personality.

"Yes, but at least you look smashing." Angie focused on the weather, on her friend, the business across the street. Anything to distract her from Coraggio on her right.

"Hold up a minute." Tori tapped on the glass and peered through the window.

Angie shifted uneasily from side to side, looking at the ground. Luna was less than ten feet away. If she pushed open the door she'd be in her arms. It sounded so *good*. Angie glanced up and met Luna's gaze through the rain-streaked glass.

Luna stood at the counter, paperwork spread out before her. She wore reading glasses low on her nose and hastily removed them as she stared at Angie. Her mouth curved up on one side in a half smile, one dimple barely showed.

The ache in Angie's chest spread and contracted, her longing amplified by Luna's nearness. Her reasons for not seeing Luna fled, along with all signs of logic and order. Angie touched her fingers to the glass, barely grazing the surface. She hurt and Luna could fix it.

"Hi, Angie." Perez stood with her arms around Tori. Angie hadn't even registered her arrival.

"Perez." Angie nodded.

"You should go in and say hi. She misses you." Perez gestured toward the door.

"We need to get to work." Angie kicked herself mentally for passing on the invitation.

"We have a few minutes," Tori gently nudged.

Angie turned back to look at Luna just in time to catch Ruby as she entered from the back room and wrapped her arms around Luna's waist from behind.

Perez narrowed her eyes. "What the fuck is she doing here?"

Angie knew exactly what Ruby was doing. Angie had left Luna alone, vulnerable. Ruby was swooping in to fill the gap. "I've got to go." Angie forced herself not to run. "I'll see you at work, Tori." She held back for two blocks, then broke into a full-out sprint. Every time she was on the brink of giving in, she ran headfirst into Ruby. How many times did it need to happen in order for her to learn her lesson?

Luna cried out when Angie walked away, "Wait!" She shrugged Ruby's hands off her, confused about where she came from but more focused on Angie's rapidly departing back. She ran to the door and flung it open. "Angie!"

She didn't expect Angie to stop, but she was still disappointed when she started running.

"Where did she come from?" Perez sounded pissed. She'd barely tolerated Ruby when Luna was seeing her. After her not-so-subtle ambush at the anniversary party, Perez's disgust had increased and her desire to hide it had decreased proportionately.

"I have no idea." Luna didn't look away from Angie's shrinking image in the distance.

"Well, deal with it, Luna. Stop letting her fuck things up."

Luna wasn't sure at this point who Perez was more angry at—Ruby for showing up uninvited, Luna for ever sleeping with her, or Angie for running scared. Luna walked inside, anger at losing the moment with Angie bubbling below the surface.

She'd been upset with Ruby at the party, but willing to chalk it up to one too many drinks. This afternoon, however, she *knew* that wasn't the case.

Ruby opened her mouth to speak and Luna cut her off.

"Save it." She held up her hand as if she could physically stop the flow of words. "Why are you here, Ruby? Do you get some sort of sick pleasure from torturing me?" Luna hadn't seen Ruby since the night at Nan and Vi's. Why did she appear again the second Angie looked almost willing to try?

"Is it so hard to believe that I miss you?" Ruby stuck out her bottom lip in a pout that Luna used to think was sexy. Now she just found it annoying.

"So call like a normal person." Luna shook her head. Ruby made no sense sometimes. "You don't get to show up here and start with the inappropriate touching."

"Come on, lover. We were good together once." Ruby took a predatory step forward and Luna stepped back. She wasn't getting trapped again.

"We've already talked about this, it's over. Period. End of the Ruby-and-Luna story."

"But circumstances have changed. I thought—"

"Nothing's changed for me. I love Angie." The first time Luna said those words to Angie, it had been by accident, a premature, poorly timed slip of the tongue. Since then the words had flowed easily and she didn't try to stop them. The audience didn't matter, only the words and the emotion they claimed.

"Looks like she loves you, too. So much that she refuses to even talk to you."

"Do you really think that reminding me of how you fucked up things between me and Angie will make me like you right now?" Luna advanced on Ruby, no longer afraid of being vulnerable. She was mad and she wasn't holding back. "You need to leave. Now."

"Come on, lover, you don't mean that." Ruby's purr lacked its usual seductive undercurrent.

"I told you not to call me *lover*." The longer the conversation dragged on, the better and worse Luna felt. She hated letting her temper have free rein. It wasn't in her nature to be mean; her mother would be disappointed. On the other hand, Ruby had caused pain for both her and Angie. It felt good to repay that, even just a little.

Before her inner sadist could take over completely, Luna backed away from Ruby. She slipped her reading glasses onto her face—a much-hated recent addition—and focused on the files on the counter. The words didn't register, but Ruby didn't know that, which was the important part.

"Go away, Ruby, and don't come back. You're not welcome here anymore." She didn't turn around even after she heard the back exit open and close.

"She's gone." Perez sounded as relieved as Luna felt.

"So is Angie."

"Tori's going to talk to her." Perez stepped up to the opposite side of the counter and forced Luna to look up. "And so should you."

"Did you see the look on her face?"

"Yes, she loves you."

Luna wanted to believe Perez, but she didn't trust her own thoughts. It was too important, the mere hint of the possibility crippling with its weight. At this point, she couldn't distinguish reality from fiction.

"I hope so."

"You should go to her."

"She's at work now." Luna had screwed up too much to add messing with Angie's job security to the list. Angie would perceive a visit at The Cadillac, no matter how short or well-intentioned, as just that. It was better for Luna to wait.

"You should join us this Saturday."

Luna appreciated Perez's whiplash change of subject, but didn't think softball would provide enough distraction for her. "Nah, my brain is so not working. I'd injure somebody with a loose ball or something."

"Oliver has softball on Saturdays, too, doesn't he?" Perez looked hard at Luna as if mentally willing her to get the message. Too bad telepathy wasn't one of Luna's talents.

"What are you trying to say?"

"According to Tori, our team is playing on the same field as Oliver's this Saturday."

"I'll be there."

CHAPTER SEVENTEEN

Saturday, September 26

"Have you called her yet?" Tori shielded her eyes from the sun and watched Oliver at bat. "Whoo! Oliver!"

"No." Between Oliver's game, Luna in the next field, and Tori's constant chatter, something needed to give.

Oliver swung and missed.

"You could always talk to her here." Tori clapped her encouragement, and Angie wasn't sure who it was intended for, Oliver or her.

Jack kept his eyes on Oliver. "What are you two talking about?"

"Luna." Tori answered, not Angie.

Strike two for Oliver.

"Really?" Jack sounded hopeful. "What about her?"

"Focus on your grandson, Dad." Angie pointed toward the field. Oliver deserved their attention.

"But she's right there." Tori pointed to the players' bench where Luna was seated. "The least you could do is wave."

"Luna's here?" Jack searched the park, his head swiveling like a bobble-head doll. "Where? I haven't seen her."

"Dad!" Angie snapped her fingers. "Oliver."

"Oh, right." Jack looked back in time to see Oliver's third strike. "Damn."

Oliver's face turned red and Angie thought for a moment that he would throw the bat. He hated to strike out, and it wouldn't have been the first time his temper got the best of him. Angie willed him to make a good choice. He gripped the bat white-knuckle tight, walked to his teammates, and set it against the fence with overt precision. Angie was proud. Self-control was better than a home run.

The coach patted Oliver on the shoulder and led him to his seat on the bench. Oliver turned and smiled at Angie. She gave him a thumbs-up.

"Tori's right, you should go say hi," Jack said.

"Not right now." Angie focused on her water bottle, wanting to move to a new topic as much as Jack wanted to hold on to this one.

"But you will," Tori said. It was not a question.

"Maybe." Angie shook her head. "I don't know."

"What's your problem?" Tori asked, much quieter than Angie expected. She didn't normally hold back even if other people were around.

Angie sighed. "You know what my problem is."

"Get over it."

"She won't wait forever, you know." Jack's pearl of wisdom came over the top of Tori's reply.

"Dad, I'm not asking her to wait." Angie said the words, but her heart protested.

"You're usually so much smarter than this." Tori looked frustrated and pissed off. "You're giving Ruby exactly what she wants. Wrapped up with a big bow on top."

Angie rolled her eyes. "You're being melodramatic."

"No, I'm not. Ruby throws one or two little punches, and you don't even fight back. If you want Luna, you need to be willing to say so."

"Do you want her?" Jack took her hand, a little too much comforting parent. Angie pulled it away.

"Yes." She answered reflexively then quickly recovered. "No." But that wasn't true either. "Shit. I don't know." She had an eerie déjà vu of their first conversation about Luna while sitting one field away. Ruby had kept her from talking to Luna that day as well.

The couple in front of them turned around and glared at Angie. Curse words at Little League games were never a good idea.

She flushed and muttered, "Sorry. Can you guys just let it go and watch Oliver?"

"You need to decide. Soon."

Angie glanced over at Luna. Their game was over and she was packing her gear. She met Angie's gaze and held it, her desire and heartbreak apparent. She took a half-step toward Angie, shook her head as if trying to clear her thoughts, then resumed her trip to the parking lot.

"You couldn't even wave to her? Damn." Tori whistled. "That's cold."

The couple glared again and Tori ignored them. Angie was grateful she didn't flip them off. Tori could be impulsive.

"You aren't running off to be with Perez."

"That's different." Tori blew an air kiss to Perez across the field. "I'm seeing her after the game, but right now I'm here to support Oliver."

"So am I."

"You're meeting Luna after the game?" Jack smiled. He was so hopeful, Angie almost hated to disappoint him.

"No. I'm here to support Oliver."

Tori pointed to the teams lined up exchanging an unenthusiastic round of good-game high fives. "Well, the game is over. How about we support him with pizza now?"

"I could go for that." Jack never said no to pizza. Or any other treat, for that matter.

Angie couldn't believe the game was over. "Who won?" It wasn't like her to miss details like entire innings.

Tori shrugged. "I have no idea. Hug him like he did, though. Okay?"

"Right." Angie realized that, but sometimes it was a good idea to know the actual score at the end of a sporting event. She waved at Oliver and motioned for him to join them. He dragged Josh along.

"Great game, sport." Jack punched Oliver lightly in the shoulder. It must have been a male-bonding gesture because Angie just didn't get it.

"We thought we'd take you to celebrate." Angie skipped the faux-punching and settled for an awkward hug. Oliver was ten, and sweaty, and not at all interested in hugging his mom in front of his friends.

"Can Josh come, too?"

"Where's your mom, Josh?"

Josh pushed his bangs out of his eyes. "Not sure. She was supposed to be here, but I haven't seen her all game."

"Come on, then. We'll grab some pizza and drop you afterward." Angie offered Josh her phone. "Call her and let her know."

"Awesome." Josh snatched the phone and tackled Oliver. After a brief scuffle, Oliver threw him off and broke into a sprint.

Angie debated yelling after them to slow down. She couldn't afford a new phone if their roughhousing resulted in damage. They were almost to the edge of the field and would stop there to wait anyway, so she held back.

Josh stopped running a few feet shy of the perimeter and turned to wait for the adults. Oliver, however, laughed when he realized Josh wasn't chasing him. He yelled, "Loser," over his shoulder and kept running, his head facing the field while his body charged into the parking lot.

Angie watched as Oliver ran into the lane of traffic. Time slowed impossibly as she yelled and reached for him, too far away to stop events from toppling drastically off-kilter. On the periphery, she heard the screech of tires on pavement and the blare of a horn, but her eyes never left Oliver's. He smiled and laughed, completely unaware of the car moving too fast to avoid him.

Oliver folded over the hood, then was flung several feet forward where he landed in a slump on the blacktop. Reality slammed the air from Angie's lungs and her legs wobbled uncontrollably. Somehow, she managed to run.

The driver jumped out of the car and raced to the front, but stopped short of Oliver. "I didn't see him. I swear I didn't see him." The woman's face was ghost white. Angie wanted to smack her. But first she wanted to get to Oliver.

She crouched on the ground next to him, careful not to touch. She wanted to scoop him up, hold him, kiss away all the boo-boos. Instead she watched, unable to think beyond repeating, "Oh my God, oh my God, oh my God."

Strong hands gripped her arms, forcing her to move back. "No! Oliver!" She screamed, kicked, scratched. She had to be with Oliver.

"Angie, honey, Luna's got him." Jack's voice, soft and reassuring, reached her. "She can help."

Luna knelt over Oliver. Without looking up she said, "Call nine-one-one."

"Is he all right?" Angie tried not to panic. She forced herself to breathe in through the nose, out through the mouth. "He has to be all right. Tell me he's all right."

"Mom?" Oliver's voice was weak, and Angie barely heard him over the rising excitement around her. She struggled against Jack's hold and half walked, half crawled to where he lay on the blacktop.

"Careful," Luna warned, pulling her into a gentle embrace. "His arm is probably broken."

Angie cried and watched as Oliver tried to sit up. Luna released Angie and placed a restraining hand on Oliver's shoulder. "Easy there, tiger. Just stay still until the ambulance arrives, okay?"

Oliver mumbled something Angie couldn't understand, then closed his eyes.

Unable to move, unable to even *think*, Angie clung to Luna until the ambulance arrived. She watched as they loaded her son onto a stretcher, careful to keep his head stable, and moved him to the ambulance. She climbed in with him and met Luna's searching gaze through the open doors. The revolving red and blue lights from the responding police car cast an eerie reflection on Luna's face.

"I'll meet you at the hospital," Luna said, then disappeared into the crowd, taking Jack, Tori, and Josh with her.

The driver closed the door and the paramedic attending Oliver directed her to a rear-facing seat. "Put on your seat belt."

Her fingers were completely numb, without strength and flexibility. After fumbling for several seconds, she felt the metal snap in place and cried harder with relief.

From inside the ambulance, the sound of the siren was surprisingly muted, the ride relatively smooth. Angie felt as though she were inside a fishbowl, distorted and confused. Maybe she was caught in the middle of a bad dream.

Dream or not, Angie wanted to wake up now.

❖

Angie smoothed her fingers through Oliver's hair. So soft. She regretted every time she'd wished he would calm down long enough for her to hold him, that he'd sit still and let her ruffle his hair like he did when he was little. Now, with him lying exhausted and broken in a hospital bed, she wanted him to hop up and run away, taunting her as he went. Of course that didn't happen.

Jack heaved himself out of the seat. "Angie, I'm going to get something to drink." He looked old. His face was drawn and tense, with dark circles under his eyes.

"Dad, why don't you go home? Take a shower. Bring me back a change of clothes." She wished he would get some sleep. It would do him wonders.

"Maybe later." He shuffled through the door, looking to the left for a prolonged moment before turning to the right. Eventually, he would find the cafeteria, or a vending machine.

Angie nodded, not because Jack was looking for some type of acknowledgment, but more as an extension of the autopilot mode she'd been functioning under since the car struck Oliver.

Not that Oliver's condition was life-threatening. Far from it. A broken arm, a bruised rib or two, a black eye, and more bumps and bruises than Angie could count. Now it was just a matter of letting his body heal and the excitement pass. She'd been inundated with a whirlwind of hematomas, contusions, and a host of other medical terms she didn't understand.

She needed a nap.

"Angie." Luna paused at the sight of her clinging to Oliver's hand. She hesitated in the door, unsure if she should go any farther. Her heart screamed at her to comfort Angie, but she wanted that attention to be welcome. If Angie found more strength in being alone, Luna wanted to give her that option. She'd waited, leaving Angie by herself with her father and son. When she'd seen Jack leave the hospital room, she couldn't resist any longer. She had to see Angie, hold her.

Angie looked up, her eyes bloodshot and drooping. "Oh, Luna." Her voice wavered.

The decision was made, Luna was at Angie's side in a heartbeat. "I'm so sorry." She wrapped Angie in her arms, careful not to hug too tight, desperate not to let go.

Angie buried her face in Luna's neck and shook against her. All that hurt and Luna had waited too long to offer solace. She swallowed her guilt and rubbed small circles on Angie's back. "Shh, it's okay. I've got you." Luna whispered words of consolation, words that, until now, seemed trite and clichéd. She wanted to find a better way to express herself but gave up when she realized this was the best she could come up with. *I've got you* said everything from Luna's heart.

"I wanted you," Angie said, the words muffled against Luna's shirt. "But I didn't know where you'd gone."

"I wanted to give you time." Luna had trolled the halls, unsure how she'd be received by Angie.

"I'm glad you're here." Angie sniffled. "But I'm not sure why you are."

"Where else would I go?"

"After the way I treated you?" Angie met Luna's gaze momentarily, her eyes shining and wet, then tucked her head back into Luna's shoulder. "I wouldn't give me the time of day if I were you."

Luna kissed the top of her head, her heart swelling. If Angie wanted her here, they had a chance, a *real* chance. Luna didn't want to blow it. "As long as you want me, I'll be right here."

Angie gripped her tighter. "Thank you."

Luna breathed a little easier. The words *I love you* slid to the front of her mind, like soldiers, silent and ready to be deployed, but she held back. The words were true. She knew it, and Angie knew it. She would have a chance later, in the quiet moments to come, to share her feelings, her desires, and her hopes for their life together.

For now, she was content to sit with Angie, who had changed, a subtle shift in the way she clung to her. A vulnerability had replaced the guarded distance in her eyes. The soft graze of her lips against the skin at the base of Luna's throat was not a seduction, but a thank you. And when Jack entered the room, Angie squeezed her hand, holding her possessively close when Luna started to move.

"So, what's the prognosis?" Luna indicated Oliver. Beyond the neon green cast on his arm, no other damage was visible.

"The broken arm is the worst of it." Angie smoothed Oliver's hair. "We can take him home when he wakes up."

Luna was relieved. For all she knew, he could have slipped into a coma. "He's just sleeping?"

"The painkillers knocked him out," Jack explained.

Oliver moaned from his bed, struggling to sit up. "Mom? What happened?"

Angie stood, pulling Luna with her. "How are you, son?"

"Feels like I've been hit by a car."

Angie sobbed and laughed. "You were."

Oliver rubbed his eyes, pulling back his arm to inspect the cast. He looked at it for a minute, then at Luna. "Will you sign it?"

"Absolutely." Luna loved him for the simple invitation. "Let me just find a pen."

Oliver smiled, his eyes falling closed again.

Luna waited, afraid now that the immediate threat to Oliver had abated, Angie would remember that she didn't want Luna in her life.

Angie squeezed her hand and cuddled into Luna, her lips close to her ear. "Come home with us. We'll work the rest out later."

Home. "Sounds perfect to me."

Chapter Eighteen

Sunday, October 11

Angie traced her fingers over the soft skin of Luna's low back, chasing the flickering shadows cast by the candles on the nightstand. Luna's body, perfect and open to her, was her favorite pastime. A new territory to be explored, mapped, and cherished time and again. Finally, she could picture herself thirty years in the future, taking the same care to learn the inevitable changes.

"Mmm, feels good." Luna shifted, bringing her body around to rest on her side. "Going to let me repay the favor?" She captured Angie's hand in hers and brought it to her mouth, kissing her fingers delicately.

"Later." Angie eased Luna onto her back and tucked herself into Luna's side, her head resting on Luna's shoulder. "Right now I just want to bask in the afterglow."

Luna tightened her arms around Angie, bringing their bodies flush. "Sounds good."

With her leg thrown over Luna, Angie's naked center pressed against Luna's hip. Every movement created delicious friction and her body flared to life. With a groan she pulled herself away a fraction.

"Really?" Luna asked, her eyes heavy and laughing. She was the only woman Angie knew who could look genuinely amused and turned on at the same time.

"Always." A few weeks prior, Angie wouldn't have dared be so honest. She refused to let Luna know how much she affected her. Now she couldn't imagine holding anything back.

"I love you." Luna kissed Angie, her lips gentle, loving, and undemanding. She'd done that a lot recently, declared her love then immediately eliminated the possibility for Angie to reciprocate. Even if Angie wanted to say the words in return, it was hard to do with Luna's tongue exploring her mouth.

When the kiss ended, Angie looked into Luna's eyes, holding her gaze in the soft candlelight. "I do, too, you know."

Luna's mouth curved into a slow smile. "What?"

"Love you," Angie whispered, the power of her emotions cracking her voice, breaking it down until she could barely force air past her lips. She needed Luna to know, needed the love to reach Luna's heart.

Luna pulled her closer, covering her mouth in a demanding kiss, her tongue exploring Angie's lips, her teeth, the soft skin inside her mouth. She pulled away with a sob. "Thank you."

"I should have said it sooner."

"No." Tears, heavy and fat, rolled down Luna's face. "You said it when you were ready. That means everything."

"Promise me…" The unspoken request was too much for Angie, dying before fully formed. She couldn't bring herself to ask for what she really wanted, *needed* from Luna.

"Anything." Luna kissed Angie's eyes. "Anything you want. I promise."

"Just hold me." Angie left the word *forever* unsaid. Luna knew her fear of being abandoned. They'd discussed it calmly, over coffee the morning after they brought Oliver home from the hospital. Saying she loved Luna was a huge step. Saying she needed her to be there, to promise to never leave, was more than Angie could manage. The weight of it sank into her chest, unable to make its way to the surface.

"Always, Angie. I'm here." Luna gathered her carefully, tenderly, as the candles around them sputtered and gave way. Luna's voice found her in the dark. "I'll always be here."

About the Author

Jove Belle was born and raised against a backdrop of orchards and potato fields. The youngest of four children, she was raised in a conservative, Christian home and began asking *why?* at a very young age, much to the consternation of her mother and grandmother. At the customary age of eighteen, she fled southern Idaho in pursuit of broader minds and fewer traffic jams involving the local livestock. The road didn't end in Portland, Oregon, but there were many confusing freeway interchanges that a girl from the sticks was ill prepared to deal with. As a result, she has lived in the Portland metro area for over fifteen years and still can't figure out how she manages to spend so much time in traffic when there's not a stray sheep or cow in sight.

She lives with her partner of fifteen years. Between them they share three children, two dogs, two cats, two mortgage payments, one sedan, and one requisite dyke pickup truck. One day she hopes to live in a house that doesn't generate a never-ending honey-do list.

Incidentally, she never stopped asking why, but did expand her arsenal of questions to include who, what, when, where and, most important of all, how. In those questions, a story is born.

Books Available From Bold Strokes Books

Chasing Love by Ronica Black. Adrian Edwards is looking for love—at girl bars, shady chat rooms, and women's sporting events—but love remains elusive until she looks closer to home. (978-1-60282-192-7)

Rum Spring by Yolanda Wallace. Rebecca Lapp is a devout follower of her Amish faith and a firm believer in the Ordnung, the set of rules that govern her life in the tiny Pennsylvania town she calls home. When she falls in love with a young "English" woman, however, the rules go out the window. (978-1-60282-193-4)

Indelible by Jove Belle. A single mother committed to shielding her son from the parade of transient relationships she endured as a child tries to resist the allure of a tattoo artist who already has a sometimes-girlfriend. (978-1-60282-194-1)

The Straight Shooter by Paul Faraday. With the help of his good pals Beso Tangelo and Jorge Ramirez, Nate Dainty tackles the Case of the Missing Porn Star, none other than his latest heartthrob—Myles Long! (978-1-60282-195-8)

Head Trip by D.L. Line. Shelby Hutchinson, a young computer professional, can't wait to take a virtual trip. She soon learns that chasing spies through Cold War Europe might be a great adventure, but nothing is ever as easy as it seems—especially love. (978-1-60282-187-3)

Desire by Starlight by Radclyffe. The only thing that might possibly save romance author Jenna Hardy from dying of boredom during a summer of forced R&R is a dalliance with Gardner Davis, the local vet—even if Gard is as unimpressed with Jenna's charms as she appears to be with Jenna's fame. (978-1-60282-188-0)

River Walker by Cate Culpepper. Grady Wrenn, a cultural anthropologist, and Elena Montalvo, a spiritual healer, must find a way to end the River Walker's murderous vendetta—and overcome a maze of cultural barriers to find each other. (978-1-60282-189-7)

Blood Sacraments, edited by Todd Gregory. In these tales of the gay vampire, some of today's top erotic writers explore the duality of blood lust coupled with passion and sensuality. (978-1-60282-190-3)

Mesmerized by David-Matthew Barnes. Through her close friendship with Brodie and Lance, Serena Albright learns about the many forms of love and finds comfort for the grief and guilt she feels over the brutal death of her older brother, the victim of a hate crime. (978-1-60282-191-0)

Whatever Gods May Be by Sophia Kell Hagin. Army sniper Jamie Gwynmorgan expects to fight hard for her country and her future. What she never expects is to find love. (978-1-60282-183-5)

nevermore by Nell Stark and Trinity Tam. In this sequel to *everafter*, Vampire Valentine Darrow and Were Alexa Newland confront a mysterious disease that ravages the shifter population of New York City. (978-1-60282-184-2)

Playing the Player by Lea Santos. Grace Obregon is beautiful, vulnerable, and exactly the kind of woman Madeira Pacias usually avoids, but when Madeira rescues Grace from a traffic accident, escape is impossible. (978-1-60282-185-9)

Midnight Whispers: The Blake Danzig Chronicles by Curtis Christopher Comer. Paranormal investigator Blake Danzig, star of the syndicated show *Haunted California* and owner of Danzig Paranormal Investigations, has been able to see and talk to the dead since he was a small boy, but when he gets too close to a psychotic spirit, all hell breaks loose. (978-1-60282-186-6)

The Long Way Home by Rachel Spangler. They say you can't go home again, but Raine St. James doesn't know why anyone would want to. When she is forced to accept a job in the town she's been publicly bashing for the last decade, she has to face down old hurts and the woman she left behind. (978-1-60282-178-1)

Water Mark by J.M. Redmann. PI Micky Knight's professional and personal lives are torn asunder by Katrina and its aftermath. She needs to solve a murder and recapture the woman she lost—while struggling to simply survive in a world gone mad. (978-1-60282-179-8)

Picture Imperfect by Lea Santos. Young love doesn't always stand the test of time, but Deanne is determined to get her marriage to childhood sweetheart Paloma back on the road to happily ever after, by way of Memory Lane—and Lover's Lane. (978-1-60282-180-4)

The Perfect Family by Kathryn Shay. A mother and her gay son stand hand in hand as the storms of change engulf their perfect family and the life they knew. (978-1-60282-181-1)

Raven Mask by Winter Pennington. Preternatural Private Investigator (and closeted werewolf) Kassandra Lyall needs to solve a murder and protect her Vampire lover Lenorre, Countess Vampire of Oklahoma— all while fending off the advances of the local werewolf alpha female. (978-1-60282-182-8)

The Devil be Damned by Ali Vali. The fourth book in the best-selling Cain Casey Devil series. (978-1-60282-159-0)

Descent by Julie Cannon. Shannon Roberts and Caroline Davis compete in the world of world-class bike racing and pretend that the fire between them is just professional rivalry, not desire. (978-1-60282-160-6)

Kiss of Noir by Clara Nipper. Nora Delaney is a hard-living, sweet-talking woman who can't say no to a beautiful babe or a friend in danger—a darkly humorous homage to a bygone era of tough broads and murder in steamy New Orleans. (978-1-60282-161-3)

Under Her Skin by Lea Santos Supermodel Lilly Lujan hasn't a care in the world, except life is lonely in the spotlight—until Mexican gardener Torien Pacias sees through Lilly's facade and offers gentle understanding and friendship when Lilly most needs it. (978-1-60282-162-0)